The Giraffes are Missing

by

Nick Delmedico

Published by

Copyright ©2023 by Nick Delmedico

Contact: halfabook@dplus2.com

All characters in this book are fictional; any resemblance to persons living or dead is purely coincidental. The Eighth Day Village of the Sun and New Maya City of Worlds are also fictional, created by my good friend Randall Rex Harrison, a man who believes that intentional communities are the next step in human growth and development. At the time of publication these places do not exist, except perhaps in our hearts. Mahalo

Manufactured in the United States of America

The Giraffe is Missing

Fiction

Action and Adventure

ISBN 978-1-58884-022-6 (print version)

    978-1-58884-023-3 (eBook version)

Introduction

Once again I find myself writing another Eighth Day Village of the Sun saga. These fantasy novels are a safe place where I can explore strange concepts wrapped in New Age thinking. The inspiration and the motivation come from someplace inside, and as long as that fountain continues to flow I will write them. Even now, another one struggles for a life of its own. It's not over yet.

Now, more than ever, we need a future we can believe in. Like R.R. Harrison, I believe Intentional and Conscious Communities are our hope for the future. We are in the midst of a spiritual awakening. On a mixed world like Earth, fear and hope exist side by side, offering each of us a choice. May your choices be wise and blessed with the best that humanity has to offer.

I have a long list of people to thank, mentors and muses who allow me the freedom to talk about almost anything and, more importantly, give me input and feedback. Jay Eklond, Sara, Raven Shamballa, R.R. Harrison, Chris Wilder, Jeremiah Hutchins, Earth Being, and of course my son, Nick, Mostly, though, I want to thank my readers. Without you, a story is like a miracle that may never happen. Without readers, there would be no authors. Without the written word, our stories and our history are quickly forgotten.

So, thank you for supporting independent authors and bookstores. Thank you for believing in the future of Intentional Communities. Thank you for reading.

Nick Delmedico
June 2023

Chapter 1
Pristine Christine

Mid-morning at Manny's Beachside Bistro is the slow time. Gone is the rush of locals and tourists grabbing supplies and a quick snack for their day's adventures. Manny busied himself behind the bar, cleaning up after the last of the morning crowd.

The sea lapped gently on the sand, the sound, as always, soothing Manny's soul and spirit. Gulls and seabirds added to the music as the sun continued to rise and cast shadows through the quiet streets of the Eighth Day Village of the Sun.

The open hut was empty save for a single guest perched on a barstool opposite him. He tried to ignore her, he couldn't say why, but she called his attention again and again until she commanded it. Now that he was staring at her, he tried to act like a cheery bartender, but like fish in a net gasping for air, the words were trapped in his throat.

She liked the shy type, found it cute that he tried to resist her wiles. She twitched nervously on her seat, staring into eyes that twinkled like they contained a universe of stars. She took a sip of her smoothie, pushing aside the decorative umbrella as she gently removed the slice of orange from the rim and placed it between her lips. She sucked the juice, squeezing the edible part between her tongue and her cheeks as she bit down with her bright, white teeth. She pulled the empty rind from her mouth with the delicacy of a bride about to be photographed. "Tell me again, Mr. DuBois, how you lost your girlfriend in a storm."

"I told you that story yesterday, Christine," he said.

"Now why would you want to hear it again?"

She leaned closer. "A girl can learn a lot about a man when he talks about his past loves." She smiled, a contagious grin that made him draw a short breath and snicker. "And what can I say? I want to learn more about you, Mr. Manny DuBois." She took a sip of the smoothie, her smile bright and warm, able to melt every bit of the ice in her drink.

"You know how we stopped a hurricane," he said.

She nodded. "Yes, with particles, pressure, and feats of superhuman strength."

"Yes," he said. He looked off to the side, almost as if he were seeing Caroline sitting on the empty stool beside Christine. Realizing that nothing was there, he focused back on Caroline, the words slowly beginning to flow from his mouth. "She was a scientist, a meteorologist. After the storm was over, she insisted on going home and working on what she called a career making paper. I asked her how long she would be gone. She kissed me and said it would probably take her years to sort out exactly what happened."

"You said was," said Christine.

"Was?"

"Was. You said she was a scientist. Isn't she still one?"

"Yes, she is," said Manny.

Christine smiled. "That's a good sign. Was. You think of her in the past tense. A sign that your relationship with her is over."

Manny wondered if there was any truth to that. "Are you saying I was dumped?"

"Relationships begin and end every day, Mr. Dubois," she said. "They say when one door closes, another opens." She leaned closer. "The trick is to hear

6

opportunity knocking at that door."

The sound of hoof beats drifted in from the distance. Manny smiled, suddenly feeling like a fish who had escaped the net. "Hold that thought," he said, turning his back to her. "I don't mean to ignore you," he said, moving to a nearby counter. "I need to prepare a mango smoothie for a very important customer."

The hoof beats grew louder, tourists on the beach turning their heads to gape at a man riding atop a giraffe. The tall beast with its mount slowly cantered to a stop outside Manny's Beachside Bistro. The giraffe sputtered and bent down low, dining on a feast of leaves in a bin that Manny kept for her. The rider was not his only important customer. High in the saddle, Randall pet her side. "Eat well, Anji," he said. "We've had quite a ride this morning, all the way to the far cliffs."

Manny appeared from under the thatched roof carrying a pole with a tray that held the freshly prepared smoothie. "You look just as hungry," said Manny. "Why don't you come down and I'll fix you a salad."

"Not a bad idea," said Randall. He twisted himself side saddled and slid down to the ground with practiced ease. Manny handed him the smoothie and returned to the prep area behind the bar.

"So, you're the famous Baba Randall, founder of this village." said Christine.

Randall took a seat beside her and set his smoothie on the counter. "I don't know if I'm famous, but it sounds like you've heard of me," he said. "You know my name, but do I know yours?"

"It's Christine," she said, extending her hand. He gently held it as he bent and kissed it. "How gallant," she said. "I haven't had a man do that to me in a long time."

"Randall is no ordinary man," said Manny. "He is our spiritual leader, head of the Think Tank."

"What's that?" she asked. "What's the Think Tank?"

"Sort of a governing high council," said Manny. "A group that helps solve Village problems and manage business with the outside world."

"You speak of the outside world as if it is something bad," she said.

"Then you misunderstand us," said Randall. "We are an intentional community. Our guiding principles are different than anywhere else. Here we value human capital over financial capital, almost the opposite of much of the world, but that is changing. There are no building codes here, yet every structure in our Village is built to withstand our worst hazards. We were recently put to the test with a category five hurricane."

"So I heard," she said. "Manny was telling me about it. He lost a girlfriend to it."

Randall chuckled, about to say something when he was interrupted.

A short, dark skinned man stuck his head between Christine and Randall. She stared at his bald spot looking like an open meadow surrounded by dense, unkempt forest. "Baba Randall," he said.

Randall slid sideways, looking around him and making eye contact with the beautiful lady again. "Christine, may I introduce my Companion Ravi,"

"Companion?" she asked, her left eyebrow lifting like a drawbridge for a high masted schooner.

"It's the word we use to describe our relationship," said Randall. "Anything more just over complicates things,"

Manny placed a salad down on the counter in front of Randall. "Ravi is also a member of the Think Tank," he said.

"Yes! Yes!" said Ravi. "Precisely why I am here. The Think Tank is meeting. Another emergency. You are needed." He turned to Manny. "You too."

"Me?" asked Manny. "Whatever for?"

"Come now Manny," said Randall. "You know you are a full time member of the Think Tank, too."

"A reluctant one," he said.

"But we need you," said Ravi. "We need our particle physicist."

"Particle physicist?" asked Christine.

"It's just a hobby," said Manny.

"Emergency!" said Ravi. "Our Sister City is gone! New Maya City of Worlds is gone!"

"Gone?" said Randall. "What do you mean? It's missing?"

"The city is still there, but the people..."

"The people are missing?" asked Manny. He looked over at Randall. "This is serious."

"Then we'd better be on our way," said Randall. He put his fork down and turned to Christine. "You might as well enjoy this salad, since I won't have time."

They all turned, about to leave, when she interrupted them. "What about the bar? What about me?"

Manny reached behind the counter and pulled out a sign. He propped it up on the bar, displaying in multiple languages, the words "SELF SERVICE".

Christine's jaw dropped a bit, her mouth making a small "o" shape.

"You'll be okay," said Manny. "I'll be back soon."

"You hope," said Randall. "Ravi, would you escort Anji to her stable for me? I'll see you in the conference room after."

"Of course, Baba."

Chapter 2
The City of Empty Dreams

"An entire city missing?" asked Baba Randall. He stared into the video monitors, a wall of screens that cycled through images from the sister city of New Maya City of Worlds. Built in the jungle, it blended into the landscape as easily as the Eighth Day Village of the Sun blended with its environment. There were open, grassy meadows that surrounded an ancient part of the city. The partial remains of old temple rose above the plain, the stone etched with the gentle age of time. Outlying structures were just as ancient, a few remaining only as partial walls and hollowed out cellars.

The old ruins gave way to the city where most of the buildings were made of native wood and stone. Beyond that, giant trees and dense jungle dominated the landscape. Here, the humans had carved out another niche. There were some structures on the ground but most of the city in this district was up above in the trees.

Wherever the trunks were still and steady, the builders of New Maya had constructed walkways, making a network of elevated highways. In a few places, living bridges had been created using techniques taught by Khasi tribesmen from Meghalaya. Trees were bent and directed, their development carefully controlled to create these living bridges. The New Mayan engineers combined this knowledge with their technology for manipulating plants and accelerating growth, ultimately sharing the knowledge with their teachers. Working together, the results were none less than spectacular, and one of the many wonders that brought tourists to the city.

Like any big city, these avenues were lined with homes, shops, and factories. In some areas, gondolas strung with cables carried goods and people across open terrain, linking stands of tree neighborhoods together. There were busy hubs with side by side, one way bridges allowing traffic to move freely across the terrain.

Randall focused on the images. Architecture, buildings, temples, trees, but no people. He turned his back to the wall of monitors, facing the assembled members of the Think Tank. "How long ago did you notice this?" he asked.

"We don't know," said Darius. "Village Operations reported it an hour ago. I thought it was important enough to call a meeting of the Think Tank."

"Yes, it was. Thank you, Darius," said Randall. He turned again, facing the monitors. Darius moved beside him and together they stared into the electronic windows with all the depth of ancient crystal gazers. A thousand thoughts filled their heads, but no psychic impressions came, no ideas that could explain an empty city.

"Where could they all have gone?" asked Darius.

"Could they be indoors?" asked Randall.

"All of them?" asked Darius. "It's mid morning. They would be up and moving around."

Dr. Stine got up from his seat to join them for a closer look. "Maybe some environmental event made them evacuate the city and seek shelter," he said. "A swarm of insects, toxic fumes from some outfall, maybe even a solar flare up?"

"We would have noticed a solar flare," said Darius. "We're only a few hundred miles away from New Maya."

"That still doesn't rule out insects or toxic fumes."

"Now where would you get toxic fumes?" asked Darius.

"Anywhere nature exists," said Randall. "Volcanoes put out toxic haze. There is something known as acid rain.

11

Then there are the mistakes made by man, be they nuclear, chemical, or more recently biological."

"Come on, Randall. Be practical," said Darius. "Acid rain could not possibly dissolve the population of our sister city overnight."

"I was just citing examples," said Randall. "However, given the strange results of climate change these days, I would not rule out an ecological disaster."

Manny was at the table. Despite being buried in a computer screen, he heard every word. "They would have notified us if they had time to evacuate," he said. "It's written into our emergency plans. We communicate and back each other up."

"True, Manny," said Stine. "But maybe they didn't have time to notify us. Whatever happened could have occurred without warning."

"You know what would explain it?" said Manny. "A neutron bomb."

"A bomb?" echoed Stine, his voice full of alarm.

"Do you think someone could have actually caused this?" asked Darius. "A name does come to mind."

"Now, now, Darius," said Randall. "Don't jump to conclusions. It's easy to cast blame on your fellow man, but that's not what we're about. Besides, the man you're thinking about would direct his efforts towards us. If that were the case, New Maya City of Worlds would be looking at an empty Eighth Day Village of the Sun."

"A neutron bomb would explain the lack of people, but I don't see any shadows," said Manny.

"Shadows?" asked Ravi.

"Remains of people," said Manny. "Residue left behind after interacting with atomic particles."

"By God," said Darius. "The mere thought of it..."

"But I don't think that's what happened," Manny quickly added. "I was just saying it to state an observation and rule out another possibility."

"Is there a neutron bomb that doesn't leave shadows?" asked Randall.

"Not that I've ever heard of," said Manny. "But that doesn't mean it doesn't exist."

"President Whiteweather may know," said Darius, He looked over at an empty seat, normally occupied by Juliana, the High Priestess of the Eighth Day Village of the Sun.

"Yes," said Randall, following his eyes. "I miss her, too, Darius. You forget she has dual roles now. I performed the wedding between her and Carson Whiteweather, and so soon after they met. What started as a challenge for her blossomed into love."

"We should all be happy for her," said Manny. "Still, I'll contact her and ask her to check with her husband and see if such a nuclear device exists."

"Thank you, Manny," said Randall. "It would be nice to completely rule out that possibility."

As Manny walked away, a man dressed as a priest entered. Darius turned to greet him. "Cardinal Jameson," he said. "What are you doing here?"

"I understand that the High Priestess is away," he said. "You are in need of a replacement. I am here to offer my services."

Darius was about to say something when Randall spoke over him. "Welcome to the Think Tank, Cardinal. You're right, we could use a spiritual anchor on our team."

"Yes," said Darius. "But can he speak directly to Gaia like Juliana does?"

The Cardinal smiled. "I talk to God," he said. "If I have trouble talking to Mother Earth, I will ask for His help translating."

Darius snorted, then turned back towards the monitors. "Maybe you could ask God or Gaia to explain this mystery, Cardinal. Save us all a lot of grief and worry."

"I will do what I can," he said. "Your priestess has been teaching me. In my hunger to study all religions, she has whet my appetite. She is a remarkable woman, and I will try to do my best, gentlemen."

"Then have a seat over there," said Randall, indicating Juliana's chair. "And do what you do best, Your Eminence."

"And what is that?" asked Darius.

"Pray," said Randall. "Pray for us. And for our sister city."

"I have a better idea," said the Cardinal. "Why don't we meditate together? Juliana tells me that it is the strength of the Think Tank."

"That's true," said Randall. "When we meditate as a group, we usually find new approaches to our challenges."

Darius scanned the room. "Where is Cameron Singh?" he asked. "Has anyone notified him?"

"He's been messaged," said Stine. "He hasn't responded yet."

"Okay then," said Randall. "I will lead. Cardinal, if you would, open the meditation with a prayer, please."

The group bowed their heads and closed their eyes, drawing slow, deep breaths as they quieted their conscious minds and listened to the Cardinal's words.

"Divine Heavenly Father, we pray for help, that we may then help others. Give us the strength and the wisdom to see the path we need to take. Let us move forward with understanding of your divine purpose, that we may support rather than hinder our mission."

Randall took over after that, his words leading them to a place where they could peacefully contemplate the problem. He droned on for a bit, then called for silent meditation. Soon, with clear minds, the Think Tank began to see new possibilities.

Chapter 3
Missing Person

Cameron Singh sat on a plain wooden bench in a peaceful garden. Water trickled in a nearby lotus pond, the white flowers floating on the surface catching mist and errant droplets from a bubbling fountainhead. Songbirds chirped, their melodies sounding like they were written by the angels themselves. White Light surrounded him, it surrounded everything, seeming to come from everywhere and not just a single source. It emanated from the birds, the trees, the lotus flowers, even the stone that made up the fountain.

His eyes were closed in meditation, a skill he practiced daily. It not only gave him inner peace, but it somehow connected him to all that he was. Recent events taught him that he might not always be able to see into every part of his inner self. Meditation at least helped him map these things, giving him insight he would not have otherwise had.

Cameron Singh knew that it is in such moments of peace, with a quiet mind, that we perceive the truth of who we are.

His skills at visualization were superb. Though his eyes were closed, he saw every aspect of the garden around him. Hearing the sound of the water, he sensed the pond. With his expanded awareness, he knew its extent. As he reached out he could feel the difference between the cool water and the dry land. When he inhaled, he could smell the lotus, mixed with the scent of the other things in his garden of delight.

A warm feeling overcame him, and he sensed the presence of someone nearby. He took a deep, cleansing breath and slowly opened his eyes.

Opposite him sat a golden being, resting on a bench that Singh did not remember being there. "Who are you?" he asked. "Do I know you?"

"You don't recognize me?" replied the Golden Being.

"Should I?" asked Singh.

"You are supposed to know everything, Cameron Singh," said the Golden Being. "You boast about being a reincarnated Atlantean, with full knowledge of your past lives. You must remember that I am also a part of your past."

"We have met before, Sir?" asked Cameron. He studied the being carefully. "Or should I say Ma'am. I'm really not sure what your gender might be."

"Does it matter?" said Goldie.

"Maybe not," said Singh. "I have incarnated as a woman before. It's not a big deal."

"What did you learn from that experience?" asked the Golden Being.

"Not much," said Singh. "Maybe that I prefer being a man. Somehow it makes me feel more powerful and in control."

The Golden Being laughed. "Have you not learned that power and control are illusions?"

"I learned that, as a woman I could still control things. I just had to use different tools and methods." He felt the eyes of the Golden Being penetrate his body and his mind. "What are you doing?" asked Singh.

"Just checking," said the Being. "Like you, I have some psychic powers. One of them is the ability to see into the depths within you and determine your truth, your fiction, and your fantasies."

"What do you see?" asked Singh.

"You still have much to learn, Cameron Singh. Perhaps as a different kind of woman, with a lifetime of no control, you may begin to grasp the truth." The eyes of the Golden Being grew bright, shining into the darkness that Cameron Singh hid from the world. It is one thing to be naked in body, but to have all your secrets revealed can be even worse. The Golden Being felt his discomfort and weakened his gaze. "For now, I see that you prop yourself up with ego. Soon it will be time to abandon this crutch and walk towards a higher purpose. I will consider your case. You would make a fine woman just as you are."

"What if I don't want to be a woman?" asked Singh.

"In your own words, what does it matter?" said the Golden Being. "What really matters is what you do and what you learn in life."

There was a ringing sound in the distance, the tolling of a church bell. Cameron Singh felt a tingle between his shoulder blades. He reached behind to scratch. "Ah!" he yelled, the tingle becoming a stabbing pain. Suddenly there was silence. The water stopped trickling, becoming frozen in time. A bird hung in mid air. The White Light which had been everywhere was now dull and fading. "What's happening?" he shouted.

"The dream is ending," said the Golden Being. "And you are needed. Don't worry, we will meet again, if not in another dream, then at the end of time."

"You haven't told me who you are."

With that, Singh awoke in his bed.

"What the... What was that all about?" he said aloud, trying to process the dream. He reached over to write it down in his dream journal. He noticed the communicator on his nightstand flashing a message. The tolling bell that had summoned him from his dream was message alarm. He checked it, the Think Tank reporting there was an emergency meeting. He took a deep breath, thinking to

18

astral project his form to the conference room, but after several tries he was unsuccessful. For some reason he couldn't concentrate. Like clouds obscuring the sun, a gloom settled over Cameron Singh as he got dressed and prepared to leave.

"Guess it's going to be one of those days," he said.

Manny got up from his computer and stood just inside the doorway to the conference room. He needed a break. Pacing sometimes helped him think. He remembered the words of Professor Huebner, his college physics teacher, giving him instructions on how to solve the more difficult problems at the end of the chapters.

"Read the problem and understand it," said Huebner. "If an answer or an approach does not come quickly, move on to the next problem. You don't realize it, but on some deep subconscious level your brain is still working on the problem. Later, when you tackle it again, you will access this information and perhaps even solve the problem. If again there is no answer, move on. Do something different. Clean house, go for a walk, take a nap, anything to take your focus away from the problem. You'll find that the next time you work on it, the answers will come."

Huebner's method of problem solving was active. His thoughts were not about New Maya City of Worlds. He thought how he didn't want to be a member of the Think Tank. He would rather be back at the Beachside bistro talking to Christine.

If only she were more like Caroline, he thought. A flush of melancholy came over him. *How can I say that? I haven't even taken the time to know Christine, despite her obvious advances. How long will I be like this? Pining away for a lost love. Imagining all kinds of hurt and rejection.* He took a deep breath, labored and involuntary.

Why hasn't she called or contacted me? Christine must be right, She dumped me.

There was a pause in his thinking before his inner voice spoke again. *Be fair about it, Manny. Why haven't you tried to call or contact her?*

He missed Caroline. If anyone was a candidate for the next Mrs. Manny Dubois, it was her.

Loneliness was something he could deal with. He had been alone most of his life. But this pining away, this longing for lost love, this was painful.

Cameron Singh came walking through the door. Manny spotted him, turned, and whacked him in the arm.

"Hey!" shouted Singh, rubbing his arm. "Why do you keep doing that?"

"I need to know if you are real, or just an astral projection," said Manny.

"I'm walking, for God's sake," he said. "If I was astral projecting I would appear suddenly out of nowhere."

"Precisely," said Manny. "You appeared in the doorway out of nowhere. Besides, I've seen your astral body walking around and been fooled by it before."

"That was one time when I came into your beach bar," said Singh.

Randall heard the commotion, turned and laughed. Manny had been doing that to Singh for some time now. He insisted that it was the only way to tell the difference between the real and the projected, and Randall tended to agree with him, "Welcome, Cameron," he said. "Glad you're here. We need your help."

"Glad to be here," said Singh, rubbing his arm. "What's the situation?"

"We've lost contact with our sister city, New Maya City of Worlds. Our monitors show the city is deserted and empty. We're trying to figure out what happened."

"I could try astral traveling over there to check it out," he said. As a reincarnated Atlantean, he had many such abilities. Like all Lightworkers, he used them in the service of humanity. "I was a little hazy earlier this morning, but I feel up to trying again."

"We were hoping you'd be willing to do that," said Randall. "It's one of the ideas we came up with after our group meditation."

"Let me relax a minute and I'll see if it's possible," he said. "I'm having a strange morning. I tried to project here from my bedroom but couldn't for some reason."

"Huh," said Darius. "I wonder why?"

"I was in deep meditation and got interrupted," said Singh. "I sometimes have trouble focusing myself after such interruptions. I'm already feeling more solid from the walk here. I'll be okay in a little while." He rubbed his arm again as he glared across the room at Manny.

Manny smiled back.

"Do what you have to, Cameron," said Randall. "Take your time. We are looking at other options."

"Could it be dangerous to astral project?" asked Darius. "What if is a radioactive event?"

"It won't affect me," said Singh. "Once I go astral, I will be in a higher dimension and unable to interact with the physical plane."

Darius chuckled, seeing Singh continuing to rub his arm. "As Manny so enjoys reminding you."

Cameron dropped his hand to his side. "I'll find a place to relax, get comfortable, and hopefully be on my way soon."

Cardinal Jameson sat at the table, his eyes closed as he said a rosary. Despite appearances, he was an active listener, whether for the voice of God or a nearby soul seeking counsel. "If you don't mind," he said, "I'd like to come and observe."

"Of course your Eminence," said Singh. "Maybe you'd like to try it with me?"

The Cardinal laughed, "Maybe another time, my friend. But I think, for now, it's more important that I keep my body here with the rest of the group."

"There's a private meeting room over there," said Darius, pointing. "Why don't you both go in there where it will be quiet." He and the others went back to looking at the monitors, discussing ideas and seeking evidence to support their conjectures. Still, no one had a viable theory of what might have happened.

Singh and Jameson entered the room and sat in comfortable, easy chairs with a small round table between them. Cameron Singh took deep breaths, repeating a pattern he had learned long ago in a prior incarnation. He slipped out of his body, expanding until he found himself looking down at his restful form. *We have many bodies,* he thought to himself. *All we have to do is focus on them. I've awakened on other planes, higher forms of existence. I wonder how infinite we really are.*

He could see Jameson studying his physical body, taking his role as an observer seriously. For a moment, Singh thought the Cardinal spotted him as Jameson turned up and looked directly at him floating near the top of the room. Singh nodded to him and smiled. His astral form drifted up and out through the ceiling. He floated higher and higher, rising above the Eighth Day Village of the Sun. With the speed of thought, he traveled over the mountains and east, past the agricultural farms that fed the Village. He flew over the airport, a necessary link between them and the rest of the world. He stretched his arms out, humming like an airplane, playfully gliding past the flying ships that brought the students, tourists and curious visitors to this sacred place. Ahead, a thick expanse of jungle lay between him and New Maya City of Worlds. He thought of the adventures and the excursions he had in those jungles and his desire to continue to explore the treasures that quietly lay hidden below this carpet of green.

His attraction to the land had something to do with a prior life he had as a young Aztec priest called Ixpetz. Like many of the tragedies of history, his people were conquered by invaders and subjugated to a life fit for slaves. The sacred temples were plundered for their gold and crystal jewels, the priests murdered, and the sacramental cacao and alter drugs stolen. Many thought it was because the priests became corrupt. They said that the Gods turned away from the people but it was really the people who turned away from the Gods.

He began to see the familiar landmarks that told him he was approaching New Maya City of Worlds. He thought of his friend Anton, who he liked to visit often, a man who made dyes out of jungle plants. He was a clever fellow who had an innate knowledge of chemistry.

Natural clothing was one of the things the City produced in abundance. Using plant fibers and organic dyes, the clothes were more in harmony with the people that wore them. Special fabrics were made for those who suffered with allergies to plastic fibers, artificial scents, and chemically manufactured dyes. New Maya fashion designers rivaled any of the big design houses of the world, often surpassing them as they set new trends. Artists experimented and made clothes that had panache, ageless in design and functionality.

Ahead Singh saw a barrier of sorts. *There's something surrounding the city*, he thought. *Like a bubble of protection.* It looked like static on a television screen. He thought about his friend Anton again, concentrating on a mental image of him. It was one of the techniques he used, an effective way to direct his astral body toward a given destination.

Back in the small meeting room, Cardinal Jameson watched the silent form of Cameron Singh breathing with slow shallow breaths. For all he could see, the man was sleeping or meditating. There was an occasional twitch, but nothing really noticeable, He resisted the urge to talk to him, keeping the many questions he had to himself.

Singh was twitching again, more violently than he had a moment ago. The Cardinal became worried. He left the room. Without interrupting the discussion among the Think Tank, he managed to catch the attention of Darius. "Excuse me," he said softly. "Something is happening."

They both returned to the room. Singh continued to twitch uncontrollably, shaking like an epileptic having a grand mal seizure.

"Is this normal?" asked the Cardinal.

"I don't know," said Darius. "I've never seen him like this."

"What is it?" asked the Cardinal.

They watched the Atlantean shake, his body vibrating faster and faster until it was moving quick like the wings of a hummingbird. His image suddenly blurred, and in an instant, Cameron Singh was gone, his body dissolving in a mist that vanished like a cloud in the wind.

Chapter 4
What Now?

"Cameron is gone," said Darius. "His body just disappeared." The Think Tank had come together again, seated around the main table as they discussed and analyzed what had happened.

"Are you sure he wasn't just projecting?" asked Stine.

"It was the real Cameron," said Manny. "You saw me hit him on the arm when he walked into the room."

"True," said Randall. "Then how do we explain the fact that he is no longer here?"

"I can't," said Darius.

"His body started vibrating, then he just disappeared," said the Cardinal. "Darius and I both saw it."

"Could it be another of his Atlantean powers?" said Manny. "One we haven't seen?"

"That is a possibility," said Stine. "He could have somehow teleported his body to New Maya. I wouldn't put it past the man. He's capable of almost anything."

The Cardinal pointed to the wall of monitors flashing images from New Maya City of Worlds. "I'll keep an eye on these pictures. Maybe I'll see him appear on one of them."

"Good idea," said Randall. He turned to Manny. "Do you think the disappearance of Cameron's physical body is related to what's happening in New Maya City of Worlds?"

"I'm not sure," said Manny. "It could be."

"What do you suggest we do?" asked Randall, scanning the faces around the table. "I had hoped that

Cameron would be able to tell us something. We are no closer to solving this mystery than we were a hour ago."

"Maybe astral travel is the wrong approach," said Manny. "Why don't we send an expedition to investigate?"

"Could that be dangerous?" asked Randall. "Look at what happened to Singh."

"How else are we going to find out what happened there?" said Manny. "Maybe we'll find Cameron there. If he's somehow been transported or teleported to New Maya, he'll probably need a ride back."

"About this expedition," said Randall. "Who would you suggest to lead it?"

"I'd be willing to do that," said Manny.

"You have a plan?" asked Darius.

"I thought I'd take one of our dirigibles. Load it up with supplies, radiation proof suits, scientific instruments, cleaning gear, anything I think I might need."

"New Maya may have many of the things you need," said Darius. "Keep that in mind."

"Are you going alone?" asked Randall.

"I want to take one or two fellow scientists from our research center," said Manny. "Subject matter experts that may be able to help. We tried astral travel, how about we try actual travel?"

"If you're willing," said Darius. "I'll have the hanger prepare a ship for you."

"Take Barclay McKenner with you," said Randall. He looked over at an empty chair, the place Barclay sat when he attended Think Tank meetings.

"Where is he today?" asked Manny.

"We're not sure," said Darius. "He checked in not long ago but said he was busy. He said he's be here as soon as he could. I'll contact him and ask if he'd be willing to help you with transportation. He's qualified and has a class two rating for operating an airship."

"Good choice then," said Manny, "Tell him he can pick two more to come with him as crew or advisors, whatever he needs. I'll assemble my people and meet him at the airship hanger on the other side of the crystal mountain."

"We'll look for you to arrive in the town square at New Maya," said Randall, turning his attention back towards the monitors.

"There's something funny about these pictures," said the Cardinal. "I've been watching them cycle through for some time. Every now and then I see a blank screen. What could cause that?"

"I noticed that too," said Darius. "Some technical issue, maybe a monitor that needs servicing." He got up from the table to join them. "I'll look into it. For the moment there are more pressing issues than a glitch in the system."

"Then I'm off," said Manny. He picked up a communicator and adjusted the controls. "I'll be on emergency frequency 2B." Without waiting for verification he turned to leave the room.

"Wait," said Cardinal Jameson. "I'm coming with you."

"Are you sure?" asked Manny. "Why?"

"Cameron Singh is my friend, for one," he said. "And I must admit that I am also curious."

"Welcome aboard then," said Manny. "Faith and Science go hand in hand."

Stine joined Randall and Darius staring into the wall of monitors. Ravi stayed at the table looking worried. "Not much we can do now," said Randall. "We can pass around ideas all day long, but without any data we are blind."

"Let's hope this expedition sheds a little light, then," said Stine.

Chapter 5
Psychic Chemistry

Manny entered the low, flat building that was the research center. He followed the signs to the chemistry department, stopping in front of a door marked "Laboratory." He could hear sounds of activity on the other side. He knocked and patiently waited.

A young man opened the door. "What is it?" he whispered.

"I need to see Professor Barnheart immediately," said Manny.

"He's in the middle of an important lecture," said the young man. "I'm Samuel, his research assistant."

"Sorry to disturb you, but we have an emergency on our hands," he said. "I'm here representing the Think Tank. We need the Professor's help."

A voice came from inside the room. "Let him in, Samuel."

"Yes, sir." The research assistant stood aside, holding the door wide open.

The room was much like any teaching laboratory, rows of tables facing a raised counter. Samuel took the nearest seat. The room was half full, eager students focusing on every word the Professor had to say. Manny stood patiently by the door, his attention, like them, focused on Barnheart.

The Professor stood behind the counter, a whiteboard of equations and chemical formulae behind him. It looked like some kind of mad graffiti found on the wall of an abandoned building. The Professor pointed to a symbol, a small triangle over an arrow that pointed left to right, the centerpiece of a chemical equation. "This symbol represents heat, the form of energy used by the chemicals to achieve the transition state. This transition state is a temporary, high energy compound that, in this case, lasts nanoseconds. It is a combination of the things on the left side of the equation, the reactants, and at the same time a combination of the things on the right side, the products. Once this high energy compound is present, it can be directed to form other products in the reaction. Remember what I said earlier, the ingredients absorb the energy, form the transition state, and then release energy as they degrade into the final products." He emphasized this point by underlining the right side of the chemical equation. He then erased the small triangle. "What happens if we remove the heat? Does the same reaction occur? And what about the transition state?"

There were blank stares for a moment. "Come on now. Think! What if we use another form of energy? Will we get the same products?"

"We often use light as a form of energy," volunteered a young lady. "So does nature, in the form of photosynthesis."

"Excellent, Miss Mathews," said the Professor. In place of the triangle he drew the letters hv over the arrow, the symbol for photon energy. "We know that light energy can influence a chemical reaction. The products we get depend on the energy of the photons and the transition state that the energy creates." He erased the right side of the equation and wrote chemical symbols for two new products. "Anyone else?"

"Electrical," said someone. "As in ionic chemistry."

"Ultrasound," volunteered another. "Often used to clean and break down grime."

"Pressure," said another. "The same way loose carbon bonds of coal can be crystallized to form diamonds."

"Good, good," said Barnheart. "Now you're all thinking."

There was a pause of silence. "Anyone else?" asked Barnheart.

"pH?" said a nervous voice in the back.

"That might be considered an ionic reaction," said Barnheart. "Mr. Hausman, I believe, mentioned that already."

There was silence again before Manny spoke up. "Radiation," he said. "As in fissionable materials."

Barnheart smiled and winked at Manny. "You may be familiar with my colleague, Professor Dubois. He teaches particle physics. Of course he would choose this method."

"And what method would you choose, Professor Barnheart?" asked Manny.

Barnheart laughed. Manny had set him up perfectly. "Glad you should ask." He turned to the whiteboard and erased the hv, replacing it with a ψ, the symbol psi. "What if the source of energy was our psychic power?"

There were some nods of understanding, including Manny, who winked back at Barnheart as he pointed his chin toward the door.

The Professor nodded. "I will leave you with that thought," he said. "My research assistant Samuel will demonstrate today's lab exercise by using his own psychic energy to drive a simple reaction. I want all of you to try it. When you think your reaction is complete, analyze it, and submit your GCMS results to support your lab work. I will expect your lab reports next week when we all meet again."

"Professor, what if we can't generate enough psi energy?" asked a student.

"Come now, Nathan," said Barnheart. "It should be no problem if you have been doing your homework. Surely you have been practicing, using your psychic powers to dissipate clouds, increase the temperature of liquids, and control the shape of water." Barnheart laughed. "Oops! Did I just give you a clue on how to complete this laboratory exercise?" He pointed to Samuel who got up and moved to take his place. "Now, if you'll excuse me, I must leave you in Samuel's capable hands. Remember, these are not new ideas. The alchemists of old used these same techniques to create gold from lesser elements. That, of course, is an advanced technique, far above your current level of study, so keep practicing."

Manny greeted him warmly, escorting him outside the room where they could talk better.

"What's so urgent, my friend, that you had to come here and interrupt my class?" asked Barnheart.

"I need your help," said Manny. "We need your help. The Village needs you."

"Calm down Manfred," said the Professor. "Whatever it is, I'm here to help."

"Please don't say that," said Manny.

"But I want to help. I really do," said Barnheart.

"I know you do, but what I mean is, please don't call me Manfred."

"But I've always called you Manfred. Even when you were one of my students."

"And I've always asked you not to," said Manny.

"It's quite a respected name," said Barnheart. "Very scientific, very artistic. It means strength and peace. Lord Byron devoted a whole tome to that name."

"What if I called you Maximilian instead of Professor Barnheart?" asked Manny.

"That would be appropriate," said Barnheart. "Call me that if it will help you adjust to me calling you Manfred."

"Look, only my mother called me that and only when I was in trouble."

Barnheart laughed. "Okay. What do you need from me, *Manny*?"

Manny quickly briefed the Professor on the situation. "Now, is there anyone else you think we should take with us?" he asked.

"How about the Gorgofsky twins?"

"The Gorgofsky twins?" spat Manny. "You mean those two psychic twelve year olds?"

"You asked me who else I would bring."

There wasn't much time to think about it. "Fair enough," said Manny.

"I'll contact them immediately and have them meet us.... Where?"

Manny, Barnheart, and Cardinal Jameson took the tram to the hanger bay, traveling through the narrow pass that led to the agricultural valley and the airport. Beyond the fields of food crops and grains was a massive hanger, home of the crystal airships sometimes used by the community to transport goods. They were met by Barclay McKenner, another member of the Think Tank, along with the Gorgofsky twins. Petra and Yorgi.

"Thanks for piloting the dirigible," said Manny. "I didn't know your skills included a pilot's license for these things."

"Are you kidding?" said Barclay. "I'm glad to be on this adventure. Thanks for asking me along."

"It was Randall's suggestion. He said you're expertly qualified for this," said Manny. He turned to his crew, an old Professor, an aging Cardinal, two young kids, he and McKenner. The sitting area was crammed with supplies, instruments, and needed materials. He wondered why they had not yet been stowed in lockers in the rear of the ship. Like his crew, this expedition had been put together quickly, and he chalked it up to that. Barely an hour had passed since he had suggested it to the Think Tank. He saw no reason to delay any longer. "Before we lift off, I'd like to say a few words, but first, if you would Cardinal Jameson, a prayer, please."

"Of course." The Cardinal lowered his head. "Divine Heavenly Father, bless us on our mission to save our brethren, to find whatever fate they have succumbed to. Protect us with angels and archangels, that we may go safely to where we are needed. And most of all, give us the faith and the wisdom to meet and understand whatever it is we find there."

"Amen," said Manny. He took a deep breath, "The Cardinal said it all. I don't have much to add, except we face the unknown, and whatever happens or whatever we encounter, thank you all for volunteering to be here with me on this mission."

He turned to the pilot. "Okay Barclay, get us under way."

McKenner went forward to the cockpit and took up his position at the controls, Manny followed him, standing beside him and watching the operation of the airship with great interest. Above, the overhead doors slid back revealing a bright sky. The giant crystal ship sprang to life, rocking gently as it slowly rose up and into the atmosphere. Barclay turned the ship, piloting it further up and west, over the mountains and back towards the Eighth Day Village of the Sun.

"You're going the wrong way," said Manny.

"No I'm not," said McKenner. "I'm going to pick up two more passengers. I need my support crew."

"Okay," said Manny. "Carry on."

Christine sat alone at the bar dabbling her fork in the half eaten salad. She had been waiting over an hour for Manny to return. "I don't know how many people are missing in New Maya, but I can tell you the name of one person I'm missing here." Perturbed, she went behind the bar, poured ice in a blender and fixed herself a mixed drink of coconut rum and fruit juice. She picked the largest glass she could find, big enough to hold the entire blender. "Might as well go all the way," she said, adding a slice of pineapple, a cherry, a straw, and a small paper umbrella. She turned and set it on the bar.

A man entered the bistro, his smile as bright as the noonday sun. His hair was wet and his bathing suit dripped water on the clean floor. His skin was tanned, tufts of hair showing beneath the towel over his shoulder, He took it and dabbed the dampness off his face. Opening his eyes, he spotted the drink on the counter. "Wow," he said. "I'll have one of those."

She smiled back. "Take that one," she said. "It's fresh. I can fix another."

He didn't argue. Lifting the glass to his lips he drank deep and long, the icy mixture sliding down his throat like a glacier in summer. "I haven't seen you here before," he said. "Usually it's that guy Manny."

She chuckled, thinking she would play along with him. "He's not here right now. Some kind of emergency. I'm filling in for him until he returns." For the moment, the blender drowned out any hope of conversation. He took another deep drink trying not to look obvious as he eyed her every movement.

"I'm David," he said, setting his glass back down. "I didn't catch your name."

"Christine," she said.

"What time do you get off work, Christine?" he asked.

She turned, surprised. "My, you move fast," she said,

placing her own drink beside his. "Cheers," she said, tapping the rim of his glass.

"Time is short," he said. "And you look like the kind of woman who shouldn't be alone. At least, not for long."

"I don't know exactly what you mean by that," she said, taking a sip of her drink. "What kind of woman do you think I am?"

"Single," he said, leaning closer. "Adventurous. Not afraid to take a risk."

"And what makes you think I'm all alone and single?" she asked.

"You have that look in your eye."

She squinted.

"No," he said. "Not that look. When I walked in here you looked hungry."

She pointed to the remains of the salad on the bar. "Not anymore," she said. "I just finished eating."

"Too bad," he said. "I was going to ask you to join me for lunch."

"You still can," she said.

"All right, then..."

There was a commotion outside, the sound of voices, ooohs and ahhhs that drew their attention away from the conversation. "What now?" she asked.

"Something's going on," he said. He picked up his drink and walked outside. The bistro suddenly looked cold and empty to her.

"Men," she muttered. "David." She said his name flatly, as if looking for it in a filing system. After a moment's pause, she shook her head and added. "You're probably as shallow as the kiddie pool at the Reiki Spa and Resort." She took her drink in hand and went outside onto the hot, sandy beach. Tourists and locals were gawking, pointing up at the sky. She twisted to see what was so fascinating.

A dirigible was approaching, flying over the mountains and towards the sea. It was beautiful, a crystal ship that defied description. You could see right through it, floating in the sky like a transparent jellyfish.

"I've heard about these things," said David, coming up beside her. "It's rare to see one." He gave her a look that told her he was the hungry one.

She had no desire to become his noonday buffet. She did little more than acknowledge his presence, letting him know that she was no longer interested in what he was selling. There was a lounge chair nearby. She walked over, sat down and reclined, taking a sip of her drink and enjoying the feeling of warm sun and icy cold drink all at once. The sea was calm, waves lapping gently against the sand. She saw dolphin leaping in the distance. The sounds of children playing drifted up from the shoreline. She took another sip of her drink, the rum beginning to warm her while the ice chilled her brain. This was truly paradise, and at the moment she didn't need anything else: no men, no tasks, no worries and no struggles.

Gawking tourists began to squabble around her, their cackle growing louder. She turned, seeing that a crowd had formed on the beach. She followed their gaze, watching the crystal ship silently drop until it hovered inches above the waves. She could see the people inside the ship moving about. "Now that's where I should be," she said. "On that magnificent airship, seeing the Village from above."

She imagined herself aboard looking down at the beach and at the languid tourists and villagers staring up at her in envy. *I wonder how I could book a tour on one*, she thought.

The ship hovered just beyond the surf line inches

above the sea. A door opened on the side. She squinted, spying Manny as he waved to her from inside the ship.

Aboard the airship the Gorgofsky twins looked down into the water through the transparent floor of the crystal ship. Below they could see fish, rays, sea snakes and coral reefs, an intentional community unlike no other, built by Mother Nature herself.

"Deploying the siphon," shouted Barclay, tapping a control on a panel. A large tube fell out of the back, one end plunging into the ocean with a loud splash. It began sucking up sea water to fill a tank in the rear of the craft. "Stabilize the ballast," came his next order, and the floating craft readjusted itself to level as it compensated for the weight of the water.

"What are we doing?" asked Manny.

"Come over here and hold these controls steady," he said.

"Me?" said Manny. "I don't know how to operate this thing."

"Don't kid me," said Barclay. "You've been staring over my shoulders ever since we took off."

"I was just being curious."

"Get over here. Now!"

Manny looked away from Christine and focused on the ship as Barclay passed control to him. He added a few simple instructions, all of them things Manny had observed and deduced. Barclay went rearward and opened a hatch, shouting gibberish and high pitched squeaks to no one in particular.

"Eh?" said the Cardinal. He turned to Professor Barnheart. "Is he talking in tongues?"

His gibberish was answered. Two dolphin leaped above the surface, landing on their backs and splashing the airship with their fins.

"Good to see you too," said Barclay. "Now get aboard. We haven't a moment to lose."

With an amazing display of power, one of the dolphin dove deep, then flew out of the ocean and up into the dirigible, landing in the tank of seawater.

The twins laughed with glee. Barnheart and the Cardinal were breathless. Barclay turned and explained. "He used to work at one of those marine parks doing tricks."

"Impressive," said the Cardinal.

"He puts on quite a show," said Professor Barnheart.

A second dolphin performed the same trick. The two of them settled into the tank as it continued to fill with seawater. McKenner went to a wall panel, flipping switches and adjusting controls. A stream of bubbles filled the tank. "It's more for comfort," he said. "Dolphin are mammals. They breathe air through a hole in the top of their heads."

"I see," said the Cardinal.

The twins were beyond intrigued. They stood close to the glass wall, watching the dolphin with interest. "Who are they?" asked Yorgi.

"Neptune and Penelope," said Barclay.

"That's not their real names," said Petra, Yorgi's twin sister.

"No, it's not," said McKenner. "It's what I call them."

"The boy's name is Amanhatayotep," said Petra.

Yorgi's eyes narrowed in concentration. "And the girl is Valencia," he said.

Jameson and Barnheart felt their jaws drop. They didn't know what to say, and after a pause of silence, Barclay said, "Well, now that we have all of our team, I'll leave you all to continue getting to know each other." He smiled and nodded, moving forward and through the door into the pilot's cockpit.

"This thing is easier to control than it looks," said Manny.

"Good," said Barclay. "Take us up and over the crystal mountain while I lay in a course for New Maya City of Worlds."

Manny pulled on a throttle. He took one last look at the beach, at Christine sitting up in her lounge chair staring in disbelief. He could almost hear her words as the ship rose up and into the air.

"Wait for me," she called. "I want to go too. I can perform tricks, better than any dolphin."

Chapter 6
Singh For Me

Cameron Singh tried to focus. There was static all around him. He studied his environment, trying to make sense of the void he was floating in.

"I wonder if this is what a character in a computer game feels like," he said aloud. "After the system has been turned off, of course."

He heard a voice in his head. "That's a pretty accurate description of it."

"I know you," said Singh. "Your voice sounds familiar."

There was a tap on his shoulder. He turned, looking into the eyes and face of his friend, Anton the dye maker.

"I was on my way to see you," said Singh.

"And here I am," his friend replied.

"What are you doing here?" asked Singh.

"The same thing as you," said Anton.

"Really?" said Singh. He again tried to make sense out of the situation, but the empty, static environment clouded his thoughts. "And what am I doing?"

"I was about to ask you that," said the dye maker. "We are all here, but for different reasons. What are you doing? Why are you here, of all places?"

Singh thought for a moment. "I don't know what I am doing or why I'm here," he said. "I don't even know how I got here, or where I am for that matter."

"Oh," said Anton. "Simple. You're standing in the doorway to the Point of Departure. Once inside, you can go almost anywhere. It's a matter of timing and finding the right wave. Which reminds me, I've got to be off. I've got things I'm trying to accomplish here before I move on. But it's so good to see you. I'm glad you're here. It's an amazing opportunity. You'll see!"

"Wait," shouted Singh. "I'm kind of confused. Which is the way out of here? How do I get out of this... doorway?"

"Oh," said Anton, a bit surprised. "I thought you knew. Just head up and into the Light." With that, his friend dissolved, a ghostly figure dusted with starlight. Singh watched tiny, glowing atoms that he left behind slowly dissipate into the gray and quiet static.

"What now?" asked Singh.

He heard the voice of Anton in his head again. "Just head for the Light."

He looked around. The gray static was everywhere. It had no source of light, no direction that he could fathom. The reincarnated Atlantean thought about it, and suddenly he knew what his friend could have meant. As he had done so many times before, he calmed himself and began to meditate.

Like all spiritual beings, Singh knew that the only true source of Light came from within, from the Light of the Soul and the Light of Divine Source. God energy may be everywhere, but Light comes from within.

With the slight effort of a simple thought and a strong desire, Cameron Singh closed his eyes and sank deep into himself, allowing the meditation to take him where he wanted to go. Inner peace and a calm, grounded center replaced his worry and confusion. Soon, when he opened his eyes again he had emerged from the gray cloud of colorless static.

He had a strange feeling. He had changed into an unfocused consciousness which seemed to occupy no particular space. He had crossed some kind of transitional barrier as he passed into the Light. He had awareness, but no form. It was not like he was astral traveling, this was something of a higher order. He could remember once having a body. He knew that it had limbs, a head, and a brain for central processing. What eluded him now was the feeling, the pulse of life, the yin-yang of breathing, and the general fatigue that builds in our body as we struggle against the forces that erode and push against our best efforts.

That body was gone, and with it, he felt free. *I must be dead*, he thought. *I don't know where I am, but I am certainly glad to be here.*

He felt comfortable, at ease and happy. Adjusting to this new environment, he started to slowly become aware of people around him. He couldn't exactly say that they were people. They appeared to have two legs and two arms and a head atop a ball of light. They looked more like five pointed stars, shimmering as they changed, becoming blobs of bright light, then pointy things as they expanded into larger shapes.

They are coming towards me.

The light shining from them was soothing. He thought of his mother. She was a saint, filled with so much love that it overflowed like an alluvial river that nourished everything that touched her. He tried to talk to the star beings but found he had no mouth. Nonetheless, they responded as if he had. In lieu of ears, he heard their thoughts, or more like sensed them. There was a moment of confusion as Singh allowed the seeds of doubt to block his senses.

Am I imagining this? The thoughts in my head have always been my own. I know when I am being telepathic, but this is different. How can these undulating shapes be talking to me?

The three blobs of light merged into one, becoming a single, glowing, pulsating star. As the points extended, they broke into beams at the tips, and when they retracted again, they formed fingers, the fat stalks shrinking into limbs. The point at the top of the star grew bulbous, a neck extending until it formed a head. The bright white light that had been a calling card faded, a shade of brown now covering the humanoid shape. Colors shifted on the surface until it settled on a golden hue that seemed to hold the light, and at the same time project it.

Singh squinted, realizing that he himself was no longer a shapeless form, that he now had a body, complete with mass and a presence. "Who are you?" he asked.

There was no need to wait for a response. The Golden Being looked down on him smiling.

The area around them cleared completely, changing in a wave of colors. Singh could now feel sunlight touching his skin, a warmth that brought with it a slight breeze, tropical and fragrant with delight. There was a scent of familiarity, of someplace he had been before. He breathed it in, the intoxicating smell of nature at its finest. *I have lungs again*, he thought. *A body!* He heard the sound of trickling water, saw the lotus floating listless on the surface of the nearby pond. With his body materialized, he felt the hard, wooden bench beneath him, the soft sand as his feet dabbled on the ground in front of him.

"I know this place," he said.

"Yes. My garden of soulful delights." said the Golden Being. "Welcome back."

Chapter 7
Unusual Skills

The airship flew high above the plains, powered by wind, guided by powerful instruments and held aloft by a hybrid of lighter than air and anti gravity technology. Barclay McKenner stood back and watched Manny manipulate the controls. "You're good at this," he said. "You should take the ground school and apply for an operators license. There aren't enough of us in the Corps."

"I might consider it," said Manny. The dirigible demanded all his attention. The controls were simple. It was the display of flashing lights, switches, and dials that baffled him. "What about all these things?" he asked, indicating both the dashboard and the array of stuff on the wall behind him.

"That's why you need the ground school," he said. "Look," he said, pointing at a compass. "Just keep us on this course. I need to go back and check on our passengers."

"And your team," said Manny. "If I had known you were bringing dolphin along as observers..."

Barclay interrupted him, all serious and full of intent. "They are not observers," he said. "And what about you? You brought two children."

"They're teenagers," said Manny. "Fourteen years old. And Barnheart brought them."

"Well, Neptune is older than that," spat Barclay. "He's older than you and I combined. Older than Barnheart or the Cardinal."

Manny stood silent for a moment. "Okay. I can see

how strongly you feel about this." More uneasy silence followed until he said, "I don't know what happened to you during the hurricane. All I know is you were lost at sea and somehow the dolphins helped you survive. I see your attachment to the animals, but are they really necessary for this mission?"

"You told me I could bring two crew members with me," said Barclay. "You didn't specify people, animals, or whatever."

Manny nodded. "You're right. I said you could bring crew."

"Okay then," said McKenner. "Keep us on course. If any alarms go off or lights flash, let me know. I'm going aft to check on my crew."

He left before Manny could get in another word.

The Cardinal was having trouble directing his conversation towards the dolphin, although he had many questions concerning their beliefs and their concept of God. Instead, he found it easier to engage the twins. "So, what is it you do in the Village, eh?" he asked them.

Barnheart beamed a knowing grin. "Go ahead, children. Tell him."

"We build the temples," said Petra.

Barclay McKenner let out a snicker. "Is that all?"

"No," said Yorgi, "We also excavate them."

"Excavate?" asked Cardinal Jameson. "What do you mean by that?"

"We help the archaeologists, the ones who find the temples in the jungle," said Yorgi.

"They also find them in the desert," added Petra.

"And the mountains," said Yorgi. He turned to Petra. "Don't forget the high mountains." He turned back towards the adults. "Often the temples are buried in rubble, or the entrances are blocked or hidden. We help move the rocks and debris. They call it excavating."

"We can also rebuild them," said Petra. "We can make them just like they once were."

"That's nice," said McKenner. "What kind of equipment do you use? You're pretty young to be certified to operate machinery."

"I know," said Petra. "They also said we were too young, the engineers and the project foreman. They wouldn't let us use the machines."

"That's all right," said McKenner. "The archaeologists and scientists also need help with the whisk brooms and shovels, too. Some digs even use toothbrushes."

"They usually do that kind of stuff after we leave," said Yorgi.

"Yes," said Petra. "After we make it safe."

McKenner stared at the children, barely teens in their early years. "What is it exactly you do at these sites?"

"I shape the blocks and he places them," said Petra.

"Sometimes when the entrance is broken and falling down, I just move the blocks away so the people can get inside the temple," said Yorgi.

"But I can also help to free them by reshaping them," said Petra.

"Wait," said the Cardinal. "You shape the blocks?"

"Yes," said Petra. "With my mind."

"How do you do that?" asked McKenner. "Chisels? Jackhammers?"

"No. It's easier than that," said Petra. "I just think about how they would like to change, and they do it for me."

"Who?" said Barclay. "Who do you want to change?"

"The rocks, of course," she said. "They have

personalities just like us. Some of them are nicer than others, and they are usually happier after I change them."

"Rocks are like people," said Yorgi. "They are happiest when they are together and doing useful things."

Professor Barnheart smiled. "The children are orphans. They came to us from Asia somewhere. To say what nation would be difficult with all the wars and political turmoil there."

"We were young when we got separated from our birth parents," said Yorgi. "People helped us escape from trouble, time and time again, I'm afraid. We crossed many borders using so many different forged papers, it's hard to say."

"I heard about them when they arrived in Mexico," said Barnheart. "I was quick to sponsor them to come and live in our village. Their help has been invaluable to us."

The children smiled, looking young and innocent.

"And Manny questions my judgment for bringing along dolphin," muttered McKenner.

"I like the dolphin," said Petra. "They are very friendly."

"You can talk to them?" asked Barclay. "I've always wanted to do that," he added.

"The twins are highly clairvoyant," said Barnheart.

"Wonderful," said the Cardinal. "Perhaps you could translate for me. I have many questions for them."

"Of course," said Petra. "They love intelligent conversation. They know you are a holy man. They are very interested in your beliefs and your concept of God."

Jameson laughed. "I was curious about the same things," he said.

"Let me talk to them first," said Barclay.

"Oh, you needn't worry," said Yorgi. "They know what they must do already. They told us everything they know about this mission."

"What?" asked Barclay in surprise. "What do they know?"

"We are coming to the, I'm not sure what they call it," said Yorgi.

"The Point of Departure," said Petra. "At least that's what it sounded like to me."

There were squeals of agreement from inside the tank. Yorgi turned and nodded to them. "They've been listening to our conversation," he said.

McKenner turned to the Barnheart and the Cardinal. "I installed sub-surface microphones there. They can hear everything we're saying."

"And what you're thinking," said Petra.

"Point of Departure?" asked the Cardinal. "But we left the point of departure already."

"Yes. What do they mean by that?" asked Barnheart.

"Only that they will try to help us pass through it safely," said Petra.

"At least with our lives," said Yorgi. The dolphin started to squeal again.

Petra turned, communicated with them, then said. "We should take seats and strap ourselves in."

"What are they expecting?" asked McKenner. "What's going on?"

"You'll see," said Yorgi.

"You'll see?" asked Barclay.

"Not my words," said Yorgi. "Amanhatayotep said that. He said 'You'll see.' He's glad you asked him to come. He and Valencia are essential to the success of this mission. You'll see."

The dolphin started squeaking, making loud noises

and flapping about violently in the tank. Everyone looked at them, wondering what was happening. Only the twins remained calm, their eyes moving back and forth like they were reading a newspaper. The water started churning inside the tank, looking like a pot of boiling soup. The dolphin began to vibrate, their shapes beginning to blur.

"What is that?" asked the Professor. "What's going on?"

"Some kind of distortion," said Barclay. "Maybe an effect of light refracting in the tank."

"I'm taking their advice, and I suggest you do too." Barnheart took a seat and put on his safety belt. "Come, children." He directed Yorgi and Petra to their seats.

"That's no distortion," said the Cardinal. "It looks exactly like the thing that happened to Cameron Singh before his body disappeared."

The dolphin squealed louder.

There was a shout from the cockpit as Manny yelled. "Barclay! Get up here right away!"

Chapter 8
Go Towards the Light

"Is this real?" asked Cameron Singh.

"Why wouldn't it be?" replied the Golden Being.

"It seems real," said Singh. "I mean. It's real in my meditation, but not like this. I visualize this garden, focus my mind, and I visit it. I even smell it and feel it. But never like this. I've never been able to reach out and actually touch a flower or feel sand at my feet. It was all so imaginary."

"Dreams are like that," said the Golden Being.

"Am I dreaming?" asked Singh.

"You tell me," said the Golden Being.

"I don't know," said Singh.

"If you thought about it, you might be able to figure it out. You are a highly intelligent, reincarnated Atlantean, after all. Or aren't you?"

"Yes," he said proudly. "I am." After some deep thought, Singh said, "I'm in a higher dimension, of course. Is this the astral?"

"Higher," said the Being.

"You're right. We are beyond emotion," said Singh. "Mental plane?"

"Almost there," said the Being.

Singh was quiet.

"You're on the soul level," said the Being.

"Remarkable," said Singh. He looked around. "The construct of this garden. How does it exist?"

"By vision and thought alone," said the Being. "Here at

this level, we can create whatever we want, be whatever we want." The Golden Being shifted, an image that blurred until it solidified again. Singh was suddenly looking at the most beautiful woman he had ever seen, the very incarnation of feminine energy. Although on a level beyond all emotion, he felt longing and desire like he had never felt before. He wanted to be with her, join with her in eternal bliss.

"See what I mean," said the woman.

"Remarkable," said Singh.

"And now it's your turn," said the woman. He watched her shift again, becoming a blur until she settled on the form of Cameron Singh, reincarnated Atlantean. "I have spent millennia creating you, Cameron Singh," he said. "Thousands of reincarnations, an eternity of lifetimes."

"What do you mean?"

"You still don't recognize me," said the duplicate. "I am your soul. You are me and I am you. For us souls, each lifetime on the physical plane is like shooting an arrow at a target. Sometimes you hit it, sometimes you don't. A lot depends on what you're aiming for. We souls practice over and over until we get the results for which we strive."

Singh nodded, glimpsing concepts that he had thought about before with his advanced intelligence.

"This is a unique opportunity," said the duplicate Singh. "We meet here in the Point of Departure, a place where all choices are possible. I have the unique opportunity to make some corrections."

"What do you mean, corrections?" said Singh. "I am a highly evolved reincarnated Atlantean."

"With an ego too big to control," said his Soul. "I'm trying to hit a distant target with a twirling battleaxe. What I need is a feathered arrow, straight and true, balanced to perfection."

"I still don't understand." Singh felt a feeling deep in his stomach, a twirling vortex of energy.

"I am taking advantage of this time, place, and opportunity to make those corrections."

"But you said I was perfect," said Singh.

"Almost," said the Soul. Cameron Singh felt disoriented for a moment. Something had happened, but he was unsure of exactly what. The Soul continued talking. "Now that my mid course corrections are complete, you can proceed to the Point of Departure and return to Earth. I must ascend to once again attend to the duties and purpose of a soul. We will meet again. In this garden if you so like."

"Please," said Singh. "How do I find my way out of here?"

"Your friends will come for you," said the Soul. "Don't worry, they will still be able to recognize you. I didn't change that much."

The Soul glowed, the form of the duplicate Cameron Singh losing all color as it turned to gold. As soon as that happened, it became light, shining in all directions, a tiny sun exploding in a supernova of divine energy. The Soul was gone and Singh remained alone in the peaceful garden. The scent of flowers and the sound of water once again crowded his senses. He sat there in stillness for an untold amount of time.

Singh noticed finally that he had shifted as well. Shock set in, seeing what his soul had done to him. He got up and moved to the pond, hoping to see his reflection. The water in the pond was blocked with lotus flowers. He cleared them away, marveling with the lifelike feel and the sense of touch as he pulled them out and tossed them aside. He looked down into an open area, but the water was dark and black.

Forlorn, Singh returned to the bench. He explored his

new form, coming to understand what his soul had done. A sigh escaped, a heavy breath that helped to carry away his anxiety. The garden began to work its magic on him. The scent of the flowers, the trickle of water, the sound of the birds, all these things and more came together to calm his troubled spirit. With nothing to do until his friends arrived, Cameron Singh began to meditate, his mind beginning to weigh who he once was, who he is now, and who his soul would like him to be.

Chapter 9
Big Trouble

Barclay McKenner took control of the airship from Manny. He tried to clear his thoughts by blocking out the sound of the squealing dolphin and the blare of the warning bells. The crystal ship was shaking now, rattling like the tail end of an angry and frightened snake. He gripped the controls tighter, flipping switches and pushing on foot pedals. There was a hum from behind him as the torus power supply crackled with more energy. Servos and gears clicked and whirred into action. Barclay bit down on his lower lip, unaware of the strain on his muscles as he struggled to hold the controls in place.

He felt Manny's hand on his shoulder. "It's okay," his friend said. "I'm here."

McKenner turned and looked into Manny's calm face. The warning sounds continued to deafen his ears, but he slowly felt like he was gaining control of the ship.

Manny calmly said, "Maybe this is a good time to explain to me what all these flashing gauges and warning lights mean."

Barclay cleared his throat and began talking as he pointed to various gauges. "This one is the power readings. We have been steadily losing power for the last few minutes. But that's not what concerns me. The proximity alarm has been ringing ever since the dolphin started twitching."

"The dolphin are twitching?"

"Yes," said Barclay. "The Cardinal said it was just like Cameron Singh before he disappeared."

"Go on. What about the proximity alarm? There's

nothing around us in any direction. Nothing I can see, anyway."

"I know," said Barclay. "The air is clear in every direction and there's nothing, but these lights say otherwise. Look," he said, pointing to a flashing display. "This tells me we are less than a kilometer away from a collision."

Manny peered out the window, squinting. He grabbed a pair of field glasses that were hanging from a hook behind him and studied the distance. "Nothing," he said.

"Half a kilometer now," said Barclay.

"I still don't see anything," said Manny.

"Should I trust you or the instruments?" asked Barclay.

"Better slow down, just in case," said Manny.

"That's what I've been trying to do," said Barclay. "That's why we're losing power. I've been trying to hold us steady, but we're being pulled ahead, into whatever it is. So far I've only managed to slow us down. The pull is strong."

"Maybe we're being pushed behind by the wind," said Manny.

"There are no winds aloft." Barclay pointed to a display that showed wind, air speed, and direction. "I can't resist whatever is pulling us. It's as strong as gravity."

Manny closed his eyes, trying to return to the calm trust that had held Barclay steady just a moment ago. Now, the warning bells and the bouncing ship were shaking it out of him. The alarms rang louder, an overbearing klaxon suddenly adding to the symphony of warnings.

"You should go aft and strap yourself in," said Barclay. "This could get rough."

"Are you sure?"

"I'm wearing a pilot's harness," he said. "It's a part of my safety gear. One flip of a switch and I'm in a protective magnetic bubble. You on the other hand..."

"I get the picture," said Manny, turning to leave.

"One more thing," said Barclay. "Please check on my crew."

"Of course," he said, again putting a firm hand on his friend's shoulders. "I'm also going to notify the operations center and the Think Tank. We need to report in."

"I agree," said Barclay.

Manny left the cockpit. Grabbing his communicator as he pulled his headset in place. He started talking into it, calling for the Think Tank as he surveyed the situation in the rear compartment. Amanhatayotep and Valencia trembled in their tank, a blur of flesh that barely held the shape of anything discernible. There seemed to be nothing he or anyone else could do about it. The Gorgofsky twins were closest to the tank, focused on the marine mammals. The Cardinal was praying, his words lost in the noise of the dolphin and the warning bells. Barnheart looked up at him and nodded gravely. Manny sat down next to him in an empty seat, still talking into his communicator as he strapped himself in place.

He looked back at the dolphin, Barclay's crew, and he wondered if they were motionless while it was the ship and everyone in it that was wildly vibrating. The surface of the water in the tank above them was oddly flat and calm. Was it a trick of light refracting off the walls and through the contents of the tank?

"Yes," said Petra, talking to the dolphin, encouraging them to do something that still remained a mystery to the others. "I agree. You must try."

They squealed in unison, high pitched sounds that echoed off the walls and deafened everyone.

56

"It's the Point of Departure," said Petra. "Everybody close your eyes."

"Close our eyes?" echoed Barnheart.

"Valencia said it, not me," she said.

An announcement came over the loudspeaker. "Hang tight everyone," said Barclay "Whatever it is, we're about to hit it."

Chapter 10
Crystal Gazing

"We are experiencing some kind of turbulence," said Manny, his voice sounding distant and canned through the speakers in the conference room.

"Can you describe it?" asked Darius.

"The whole ship is shaking," said Manny. "Every bell and warning whistle is going off at once."

"We hear them in the background," said Darius. "How far are you from New Maya?"

Stine pointed to a monitor that displayed a map. "We've been tracking them," he said. "They're right at the outskirts of town."

"The proximity warning keeps going off," said Manny. He explained the situation as best he could, telling them that they were in imminent danger of colliding with something they could not see.

They heard Barclay McKenner's voice over the communicator. "Hang tight everyone," it said. "Whatever it is, we're about to hit it."

Stine watched the monitor. The blip that indicated the airship suddenly disappeared. "They've gone off scope," he said.

The speakers went quiet. "Manny!" shouted Darius. "Manny. Come in Manny!"

"No use," said Stine. "We've lost touch with them. The communicator is dead. No signal."

"What now?" asked Ravi. "More meditation?"

"Don't be ridiculous, Ravi. Meditation won't solve this," said Randall. "We're at the limits of our imagination. What

58

we need are hard facts and concrete evidence to analyze."

"Maybe this will help," said Stine. "I was reviewing the recent entries into the New Maya City of Worlds records and archives. As you know, we maintain a series of connected computers with our sister city. They update each other on a regular heartbeat. I found this entry by one of their research scientists." He punched some buttons on his computer, directing it to a display on the wall.

A tall, gaunt man stood next to an ancient wall. "I am Doctor Candle, principle researcher for the Temple of the Sacred Jaguar. This place, uncovered recently by our colleague Cameron Singh from our Sister City, Eighth Day Village of the Sun, is a hidden temple dedicated to the spiritual evolution of our species. We have deciphered much of the writing and many of our priests, initiates, and adepts have tried the sacred drugs left behind by our ancestors. We have conservatively dated their age back 75,000 years to the existence of Lemuria. These drugs have not lost their potency, and we have noticed that our test subjects seem to gain peculiar psychic abilities once these drugs are consumed. Our efforts to analyze these compounds have failed, but we still have hope as our best chemists are working on the problem. All we know is they have a spiritual effect that cannot be duplicated by our current level of science. These complex compounds open the doors to higher perception. The wisdom of the past comes to light, and our test subjects report being clear in consciousness, purpose, and dedication to life."

"We get the same thing through meditation," said Darius.

"Yes," said Randall. "But it takes longer. Drugs have been used as a short cut to higher consciousness for millennia. Their effect is usually short lived. Sustainability is only achieved by consuming more of the drug, which can lead to addiction. Meditation is a natural path."

Stine paused the video. "These drugs are not like that," said Stine. "In my review I came across journal entries and scientific research that documented the effects of these drugs. There is a kind of sustainable ecstasy that comes about with their usage, a more permanent connection to the higher self. And, there is no need to consume more of the drug. In most cases, the effects are permanent."

"Permanent enlightenment," said Randall. "It must make it hard to live in this world."

"What do you mean?" asked Ravi.

"To be in this world and not of it is the most difficult path," said Randall. "Attuned to the spiritual. forever an outsider, forever feeling you don't belong."

"Many people who want that kind of experience renounce this world and live in a monastery," said Darius.

"Personally, I like a state of balance where I interact with the world," said Randall. "You can get as spiritual as you want, but let us remember that we have a physical body and we are here for a reason."

"True, but we have many bodies," said Stine,

"And to work on one is to work on all of them," said Randall. "The physical body anchors us in this world. When I perform a task, I focus on it fully, living in the moment, and that makes it a spiritual task, especially when I dedicate it to some higher purpose."

"Yes, Randall," said Darius, his voice sounding tedious and condoning. "We all know chopping vegetables can be an act of divine love."

"This goes beyond that," said Randall. "Think of it. Spiritual ascension. What if I asked you if you wanted to visit heaven, or even go and live there, Would you want to stay and help the Earth or humanity? Or would you be done with this suffering and gladly take the ticket home?"

"Quit the world?" said Darius. "That almost sounds like suicide,"

"Except your body would still be alive," said Randall.

"A nice debate but we're getting off track here," said Stine. "Let's focus. Doctor Candle is getting to the part I found interesting." He pushed a button and the video began again.

On screen, Candle continued. "With special permission, we had a team access the Akashic Record, the known, recorded history of the Universe that is stored in the higher dimensional Hall of Records. We found the link between the Temple of the Sacred Jaguar and the old ruins that are the centerpiece of New Maya City of Worlds. The records did not reveal anything more than that, so we were left with yet another mystery before us. This led to us poking around in the old ruins looking for answers. There was an uproar among the citizens of New Maya about disturbing the ruins. The site is sacred, and doing so is akin to digging up a burial ground. Eventually, against public opinion, we got permission and began to excavate the area.

"What we have discovered is the tip of what we believe to be a massive crystal." The camera scene cut to a picture of the crystal, a glittering white rock jutting from the ground. Machinery moved around it, ropes and pulleys attached to its body. A team of people carefully worked as they dug out a trench around the base. Candle's voice continued over the video images. "We are toiling day and night to learn more about this remarkable find. We hope to learn even more as we carefully excavate the crystal and expose it for study." The video switched to a night view, the site lit with bright lights as the activity continued around the clock.

"There have been other finds among the ruins,

passageways that lead to blocked corridors, treasures that are now being curated in our local museum. There are writings on the walls that continue to illuminate the past. We have had to stop all work in these tunnels lest we disturb the booby traps set by our ancestors. To that end, I have asked the New Maya Council of Elders to see if they can arrange for the Gorgofsky twins to come and assist us in our efforts. They have helped us in the past but were unable to rebuild the temple or even to shed any light on its purpose. Without a blueprint, we have no idea what the temple originally looked like, let alone its purpose. I have also contacted Cameron Singh about coming here. He was able to decipher the hieroglyphics on the walls of the Temple of the Sacred Jaguar and successfully navigate the traps that were there. I eagerly await the assistance to get safely through these traps.

"In the meantime, it is about this unearthed crystal that I wish to speak. Since its discovery, there has been talk in the City of Worlds about its purpose. Unlike the hieroglyphics found in the Temple of the Sacred Jaguar, we were unable to make any sense out of the small amount of writings found on the walls of the newly discovered passageways. The crystal is referenced multiple times but the message is unclear. Nevertheless, my most prominent theory revolves around the mysterious disappearance of the Toltecs in the 12th century A.D. It was originally believed they were wiped out by famine, warring tribes, and even the arrival of the Conquistadors. Although all these factors may have a hand in the decline of their civilization, they vanished almost overnight. Or perhaps, more likely, it was not at night that they vanished, but in broad daylight. Again, I refer to the markings in the Temple of the Sacred Jaguar. It is here we find another reference to the crystal." The video cut to a glyph showing a man standing beside a tall crystal. Candle continued speaking.

"We thought this referenced something we would find

62

in the Temple of the Sacred Jaguar, but no such object was found. Also, we thought the man was part of the next word, which led to a different interpretation of this glyph. Only after unearthing this massive crystal did I realize that the man was a point of reference, a model by which we could judge the size of the crystal. With this new information, I attempted a new translation. The crystal is named, and although the words are difficult to translate, I have come up with several possibilities. The Forever Jewel, the Gemstone of Eternity, The Soulfinder, and my preferred designation, The Ascension Crystal.

The screen switched back to Doctor Candle, looking haggard and exhausted. "We do not know any more than this. For the record, tomorrow is the day we finish our excavation. I file this report of our progress to date, and with it our plans to study this jewel and its spiritual purpose in more detail."

The video ended and the screen returned to cycling images of the empty New Maya City of Worlds.

"Is there more?" asked Darius.

"It ended rather abruptly, don't you think?" said Ravi.

"That's all," said Stine. "Did you notice the date the report was filed?"

"Yes," said Darius. "It was yesterday evening."

"What do you make of that, Randall?" asked Stine.

"The Ascension Crystal," he answered. "Curious name." He turned away from the monitors. "Darius, can we get an image from any of the cameras that might be facing the old ruins? I'd like to see that crystal."

"Odd," said Stine. "Have you noticed that none of the images on our monitors have shown the old temple."

"The Cardinal said something about that before he left on the expedition," replied Darius. He went over to a computer and began typing. "I'm trying, but every camera pointed towards the temple is showing a blank screen. That's why the automatic feeds ignored the images. The system thought the cameras were damaged, but a few of them got through, which explains why the Cardinal and I both noticed one." He pressed some keys and empty, white screens appeared on the monitors. "It's something weird. Not white noise and not an equipment malfunction. Something completely different. It's on every camera that was pointed at where the crystal should be." He got up from his seat at the table and joined Randall. Stine was already at his side and the three stood there, gazing at blank screens, hoping to see a crystal but instead viewing static. Only Ravi sensed something as he turned to the side and blocked his view of the monitors.

Stine, Randall, and Darius stared at the static pattern, unable to look away, unable to gather their thoughts. Ravi called to them one at a time. When they didn't respond, he went over to the computer where Darius had set up the images. With a bold keystroke, the static faded, replaced again with images cycling through the empty streets of New Maya City of Worlds. Stine rubbed his eyes as Darius shook his head and Randall relaxed his tense pose. Looking away they regained their composure.

"What was that?" asked Randall.

"You should be asking, where was that," said Stine. "For a brief moment, I was not in this room. Isn't that what you experienced?"

"I'm not sure what I experienced," said Darius. "I think I just got lost in static for a moment, the same way crystal gazers go into a psychic trance when they stare off into the infinite."

"Thank you, Ravi," said Randall. "I'm curious. What made you look away?"

"I didn't actually look away," said Ravi. "I mean, I looked away, but when the image flashed on the screen, I felt like I was falling. And that's what happened. I started to actually fall, so I looked away to catch myself. Then I saw the three of you lost in some kind of trance."

Randall walked over to the conference table and sat down. "Join me, please. Everyone," he said. Stine, Darius and Ravi took up their seats. "Well," he said. "Time to reconvene the Think Tank, or what's left of it. I need all the brain power you can muster, my friends. It seems this crystal has some effect on our world, and it may even be responsible for what happened in New Maya City of Worlds. Just staring at a camera screen took us to some other dimension. Unlike Singh, we still have our bodies here in this physical universe. I fear, if we don't find a way to fix this soon, it will only be a matter of time before this crystal grows stronger and expands its field of operation."

"What do you mean?" asked Darius. "What can happen?"

"I think I know," said Stine. "While we stared at the blank monitors, we were not entirely in this room. Given time, I believe we would have all disappeared, leaving poor Ravi alone to try to figure this out."

Chapter 11
Sounding the Depths

Barclay McKenner floated in a weightless void. It had density, and he could feel pressure against his skin. It was warm, nourishing, and not unlike the amniotic fluid that supports all emergent life.

Time stood still, yet he felt its passage. Like a watched clock, there seemed to be endless waiting filled with earnest anticipation. Of what, he could not say, but emotions are sometimes like that, general feelings with little thought attached.

He heard a high pitched noise. It cleaved the void like the beam of a flashlight in a dark room. He heard it again and concentrated on it. The sound twisted in his consciousness and he could feel it affecting him deep inside somewhere.

"I know that sound," he said. "It's Neptune. He's calling for me to come and help."

Movement through the void was like swimming in the ocean, comfortable and easy for him. He accelerated, going faster and faster, feeling the pressure against his skin as he moved through the fluid. It passed smoothly around his sleek body, creating subtle impressions that extended his awareness well into his surroundings.

In a sharp, surprising moment, he broke through some kind of membrane, almost like the surface of the ocean, but at an unexpected angle that did not line up with his sense of gravity. He shouted, startled and excited, as he suddenly felt himself aloft in empty space, airborne and floating. Below him, he saw New Maya City of Worlds. It was still empty, devoid of souls. He studied the ground below, thinking how he expected to fall now, aware suddenly of the mass of his body and the power of attraction that the Earth had for it.

He heard a squeal, the high pitched call of the dolphin. And then he felt a more powerful force that tugged at him, pulling him back through the membrane and into the amniotic fluid.

The noise was louder now, coming from all around him. A flash of memory emerged, and he knew he was among friends. Neptune and Valencia were there beside him, pointing their noses towards an unknown destination through the void.

"I wish I could understand you," he said.

His thoughts became reality.

"We need to save them," said the squeal. "Follow us."

"I know the way out," said Barclay. "We can break through the barrier here."

"Once we have the others it will take all three of us working together," said Valencia.

"And it will have to be done carefully, at just the right point of departure," said Neptune.

"But first we must find them," said Valencia. She let out a high pitched squeal and Barclay understood. The noise was functioning like sonar, like echo location, bouncing off objects and returning to his ears with the outline of something heavy and solid.

"This way," said Neptune.

"What will we do when we find them?" asked Barclay, swimming to keep up with them.

"They must be given the opportunity to choose," said Valencia. "This is the Point of Departure."

Neptune turned left, Valencia following him. He heard the echoes of their high pitched squeals. "It will take all three of us," it said.

Barclay once again accelerated, feeling a new purpose and mission. He called to his friends, his voice strong and high pitched, a call that told them he was right behind them.

Chapter 12
A Lesson for Teacher

Barnheart tried to focus through the fog. "My mind is my guide," he said to himself. "I am a scientist. I will remain calm and observe."

He shut his eyes, a technique he often used to close himself off from the world, creating a place where he could be alone to think. When he opened them again, he was in a classroom. But not any classroom.

"It's my teaching laboratory," he said out loud. "I'm back at the research center in the Eighth Day Village of the Sun." He smiled, sitting in the back row, far from the whiteboard. He squinted, recognizing the words and symbols he had scribbled on it mere hours ago when he was teaching.

"But where are all my students?"

The classroom was empty, the small workbenches arranged in neat, symmetrical order, each potentially seating two students who would share a common sink and utilities. All empty, not even a ghost to remember or repeat his words back to him.

"My whole life," he said. "Teaching everything that I learned." A strange feeling came over him as he recalled being aboard an airship with some dolphins. "So why am I here?" he asked aloud.

"To learn," came an answer. He looked up, noticed someone at the head of the class behind the lectern that he usually occupied. He stood up. Moving forward between the rows of benches.

"That's right," said the voice. "Come closer. I always judge a student by where they sit in my classroom. The eager ones, the ones who want to learn, they're always up front."

"Yes," said Barnheart. "The back row is for the troublemakers. The sleepers, the ones with recording devices, and those only vaguely interested in what you're saying."

"Are you interested in what I have to say?" asked the voice.

"I'm always interested in what people have to say," said Barnheart. "But I'd be more interested in hearing what you're doing at my place. I'm supposed to be the teacher here."

"Are you, now?"

"It says so on my credentials." Barnheart reached into his back pocket as if he carried a diploma there. Instead he pulled out a student ID, the picture much like he looked in his college days. He read the name, Max Barnheart. He looked up and saw himself at the podium, at least what he looked like this morning when he was teaching his class.

The teacher smiled. "Take a seat, Maximilian. Right up front. I know you'll want to pay close attention."

"I like to be called Max," he said.

The Professor chuckled. "So you do, Max. So you do."

"Who are you?"

"Isn't it obvious?" answered the Professor. "I'm you."

Max reared back, an involuntary movement of his body.

"Don't act so surprised," said the Professor. "You knew it all along."

"Yes, I did," said Max, hearing the truth in those words. "So, Professor. What am I here to learn?"

"You're not so much here to learn. More like you're here to remember."

"Remember?" asked Max.

"Yes," said the Professor. "Something you learned a long time ago."

Max leaned forward. "Now you have me Professor. Please go on."

The symbols on the whiteboard moved, rearranging like an animated cartoon. When they stopped, Max studied them, searching his mind for any memories he might find.

"No," said the Professor. "You have it all wrong. You're too limited. It's not something you learned in this lifetime. Think on a grander scale."

"Huh?" asked Max.

"Go further back," said the teacher. "Back before you were Max."

Barnheart, now a curious student, studied the whiteboard. He recognized his own work, things and formulas he had written over and over again, semester after semester. His research into psychic chemistry. With all that work, he had pioneered the field but done little to make a true breakthrough. Teaching had been his slow retreat, combing the front rows of his classrooms for his successor, a young student whom he could mentor in the arts. Someone who would carry the torch and complete his work.

The formulae looked slightly different. In addition to the psi energy ψ, there was a plus sign above the arrow, the added symbol ◎ appeared.

"Excuse me, Professor," he said. "What is that small symbol, the two interlocking squares surrounding the small circle."

"Good question, Maximilian," said the Professor. "Oh, I mean Max." He smiled. "You should be able to answer that question yourself. Have you remembered yet? "

Max thought for a moment then shrugged his shoulders.

"Maybe if I gave you a clue."

The Professor shimmered, his form altering in a wave of illusion, all at once dissolving and reforming into another man. This one wore a colored cloak over a simple tunic that was held in place with a belt from which hung various sized pouches. The man moved from the podium to the demonstration bench. He had a long beard and a stiff gait. He opened a jar and removed a few spoonfuls of the stuff inside, placing it on a small, glass dish. "Do you recognize this substance?" he asked Max.

Max strained, rising slightly from his seat and craning his neck to get a better look.

"It's okay," said the man. "Come forward. It's just you and me here."

Max got up from his seat, moving opposite him and studying the yellow powder on the clear plate. "It's sulfur," he said.

"Correct," he answered. "Now watch and pay close attention." He reached under the counter and brought out a metal stand. Then he brought out a crystal, shaped round like a lens, and he fitted it to the stand. "Does this look familiar yet?"

It was as if he had amnesia, a sudden moment which triggered a curious thought that soon opened a floodgate of memories. Max looked up at the teacher. "Of course," he said. "You *are* me." He said the words as if he realized them for the first time, believing them wholeheartedly. "That's the way we dressed back when we were..." The amnesia set in again and he searched an empty library of memories once more.

"An alchemist?" said the man, posing it as a question for Max to consider.

The floodgate opened again, becoming a spillway that emptied into the lake of his unconscious. And the memories were there again for him to swim through. He turned to the professor. "May I, sir?" he asked.

The Alchemist smiled. "This is why I teach," he said. "To see the moment of recognition, the birth of an idea, the miracle of learning. The magic spark that ignites the flame of knowledge and transfers it from one being to another."

"Of course," said Max, thoughts fitting together like a child's set of building blocks. "The symbol, the two squares and the circle. We used it to represent the crystal, another way of focusing psychic energy." He moved the stand and placed it before him, adjusting clamps and rotating the crystal until he had it pointed just the way he wanted.

"Yes, Max," said the Alchemist. "Go on. You were saying?"

"We often overlook the power in naturally formed things like minerals, gems, and crystals." He bent down slightly, positioning his third eye in line with the crystal and the sulfur on the glass plate.

"Wait," said the Alchemist. "Let me turn on the psi light."

"What?" asked Max.

"The high frequency light that makes our thought waves visible." He flipped a switch on the wall. Light, not unlike a black light, flooded the room. "Go ahead."

Max focused through the crystal, his mind reaching for something he didn't quite understand, but he knew would work. He thought of the Gorgofsky twins and what he had learned from them, about how the rock, like all things, aspired to a noble purpose. He looked down at the sulfur, as if getting to know it, asking it if it, too, had such aspirations. The answer came, and his thoughts shaped the destiny of that simple element. He felt the electrons interact in a new way, a familiarity with each other that they had not previously shared. In the nucleus of the atoms, protons and neutrons reached out in waves to the galaxies and universes that surrounded them. As the electrons intermingled, they were drawn together, their quantum states becoming at first waves and then settling back into particles. Barnheart put his psychic thoughts into the equation, focused through the crystal. They were lit by the black light in the room as purple rays of light shone from his forehead. The Alchemist's face glowed in the eerie beams as they struck the glass platter, surrounding it with the pure light of Max's conscious thought.

The sulfur melted and reformed, becoming a pool of liquid that slowly cooled as it leaked heat and excess energy into the surrounding environment. The Alchemist turned and flipped a switch, the black light disappearing in the normal lighting of the room.

Barnheart noticed something about the light. It was everywhere and nowhere. "Where exactly is that light coming from?" he asked. The amnesia still seemed to bar him from certain neighborhoods that bordered memory lane. "I should definitely know the answer to that question," he said.

It went unanswered. "Well," said the Alchemist, who now turned back into the Professor. "Was your experiment a success, Max? Do you want to do a spectral analysis? Maybe a qualitative analysis? The old flame test?"

Max moved the crystal aside and looked down into the plate. Time stood still with the realization of what he had done. When he could breathe again, he said in a whisper, "I don't have to. I know what it is."

It gleamed back at him, pure and refined, the base sulfur having yielded to it's higher aspirations.

He looked at the Professor, a mirror into his past. He

said the word but it came out in unison, a chorus of two voices that sang the answer together.

"Gold."

The Professor smiled. He wrote something on a piece of paper and slid it across the table. "Put that in your back pocket, Maximilian Barnheart."

Max looked down at it. It was a simple card, a large A+ ornately scrawled on it. He looked up at the Professor, about to say something. There was a loud screech from the hall. He turned and looked towards the exit door, then back at the Professor,

"I think I hear dolphin calling for you," said the Professor. "Better go check on that."

The squeal got louder. Barnheart went to the door, flinging it open to see what was there. He stepped out into the hallway and it became dark. He turned back towards the door of the classroom, but it was no longer there. He went to take a step and was lifted off the ground by a torrent of water. Clawing at it, he choked until it was all around him and in him, penetrating like something he had never felt before.

I'm drowning, he thought.

The squeal came again, loud and deafening. Max turned towards the direction he thought it came from. Again he heard it, focusing his senses. In the distance, he thought he saw a tiny pinpoint of light. He started swimming towards it, watching it grow brighter with every stroke. In his excitement, he began to paddle harder, hearing the squeals get louder as he approached the source of the Light.

And then, in a magic moment, they were beside him. Neptune and Valencia had him cradled between them, pushing through the amniotic fluid as they carried him off.

Ahead, a third dolphin led them on, squealing as he

navigated the void, searching for the next soul he needed to rescue.

Chapter 13
The Cardinal Rule

Jameson floated on a cloud. He heard music, something ethereal that he could not quite place. The sound of voices blended with instruments he could not quite fathom. Through the clouds, he thought he he saw angels.

"You did."

Beside him stood an angel, more beautiful than anything he had ever seen. It glowed, garments made of sheer light, its face a glaze of shimmering life force. "Angels always surround you," he said. "You should know that, your eminence."

"I do," said Cardinal Jameson. "I just never talked to one of them."

"But you have, Carmine Jameson. You have prayed many times to your angels, especially to me, your guardian angel."

Jameson saw a projection in the clouds, like the screen of a movie. A little boy was kneeling beside his bedside praying while his mother watched. "Guardian angel, angel so dear, who trusts me now and stays so near. Ever this day be at my side, to light my way, protect and guide. Amen."

Jameson smiled. "I'd almost forgotten that prayer."

The projection changed to a new scene. It was the insides of a church. Jameson was much older, now a young priest. His words were low and soft. "Guardian angel, I need you now at my side. Give me the strength I need."

There was a loud crash, followed by laughter.

Jameson stepped out of the shadows. The three men turned toward him, unafraid and bold. "What do you know," said the leader. He stood high in the pulpit, a place reserved for sacred sermons. "An old style padre."

His two sidekicks laughed. One stepped forward holding a large, gold candlestick he had taken from the alter. Behind him Jameson saw the broken window, a stained glass antique thoughtlessly shattered like a glass thrown into the fireplace after a wedding toast. Prayer books and hymnals were scattered on the floor, shredded like paperwork at recycling plant. A statue of the Virgin Mary was on its side. There was graffiti spray painted over a fresco that had survived for centuries, the words too vile for him to ever repeat.

The sidekick with the candle holder continued to advance, swinging the candlestick from side to side, holding it like a bludgeon. The other followed, picking up a flagpole from a stand. He ripped the cloth from the pole, the holy flag of the Vatican, throwing it on the ground before twirling the stick like a weapon, making it cut the air with a deadly whoosh.

"Oh, guardian angel, how I need you now," whispered Jameson. "And maybe an archangel or two,"

"What's that, Father?" shouted the leader.

"Answer him," shouted candlestick. His bat swung, whacking Jameson across the cheek. A trickle of blood formed. The assailant stopped cold.

A well of strength and fortitude rose from somewhere deep inside Jameson. The priest stood calm, staring at his assailant, unafraid as the swinging flagpole moved towards him for another strike. He planted his feet firmly, his posture now making him stand tall, "What do you want?" he shouted, his voice echoing off the walls and the high ceiling of the old church. "You want the other cheek?"

He turned, baring his good side towards the man.

"That's a good Christian." The flagpole spun faster, sounding like helicopter blades. Only a few more steps lay between him and a cracked skull.

It suddenly stopped, caught in the grasp of his companion, one hand on the flagpole, the other gripping the candlestick. "What are you doing," he said calmly. "How can you hit a man who faces you like this?"

Flagpole laughed. "I think he was ready for it, even wanted it. What do you say, Padre?"

Jameson's jaw tightened. "I say, this is a house of God," he said angrily. He felt a hand on his shoulder, the invisible presence of his angel. His speech softened. "I say, in the name of the Lord God, you are welcome here. Especially if you are troubled." The two men stood in shock. Jameson reached out and gently took the candlestick from the man and walked over and placed it on the alter. He returned to the man with the flagpole and held his hands out. "Now, tell me what's troubling you, my son. What pain do you hold that you must do something like this?"

The lighting in the church changed. Like ghosts materializing, angels appeared. Two stood on either side of Jameson, one with a hand on the young priest's shoulder, the other wielding a mighty sword. The man who had held the candlestick was also flanked by two angels, both smiling at him. Up on the pulpit, an archangel floated behind the leader, bright light shining down on the man from above. The shadow of a thousand priests appeared at once in the pulpit, flip book pictures superimposed over the leader, now looking stoop shouldered and defeated.

Jameson looked up at him. "Tell me what troubles you," he said. "Preach me the sermon that is your life, that I may learn from it."

The projection faded.

"I remember that night," he said to the angel. "Those men all joined the church."

"Thanks to you," said the angel.

"And you, of course," said Jameson.

The angel smiled, then pointed. "This way." he said.

Jameson was no longer on a cloud. He was in a quiet office. A warm fire burned in a large fireplace along one wall. Two chairs sat facing it, their backs to him, a small table between them. On the other side of the room was a desk, large and ornate, the pride of any CEO or corporate president. "This is my office," said Jameson, seeing the familiar surroundings. He started to head for the desk when he heard a voice from one of the chairs by the fireplace.

"Come, Carmine. Sit over here by me."

He recognized the sound immediately. "Father Kaupon?"

The man twisted, his face coming out from behind the chair to smile at Jameson. "Yes, my son. Come. Sit by the fire with me."

Jameson stood frozen in awe. "But, you passed away long ago," he said. "I was at your funeral." Deeper thoughts began to stir within the Cardinal. "Am I dead, too?"

"Sit with me. We'll talk about it."

Jameson went to the empty chair, sat and collected his thoughts as he stared at the fire. There was something enchanting about it. Like an ordinary fire, it created sparks of color, but it gave off a different kind of light and heat. It was a kind of warmth that he had never felt from a fire before. The heat went deep into his body, building his strength, healing, and making him feel young again.

All thoughts of death receded and he ceased to think about how he found himself in this setting. Instead, he relaxed and continued to stare at the fire.

An infinite amount of time passed before Kaupon said, "I can't tell you how good it is to see you again."

Jameson came to life, thoughts awakening in his head like a hill full of wild flowers blooming in the spring. He tilted forward, then sank back into the chair as he settled into gloom.

"No, you're not dead," said Kaupon, as if reading his thoughts. "Not yet, anyway."

All thoughts of death left the Cardinal's mind at those words. "Then where am I, if not dead," he said.

"This is only the Point of Departure."

"I've heard that phrase before somewhere," said Jameson. "Is this what it looks like?"

"It's different for everyone," said Kaupon. "It's just a reflection of someplace you feel comfortable. A waiting room or way station, so to speak."

"I do feel comfortable here." There was a dolphin squeal from the hallway and he turned towards the sound.

"You'll have time for that later," said Kaupon. "Listen to me for now. There are some things I did not tell you about, things I regret keeping from you."

"There were no secrets between us," said Jameson. "I told you everything, even about the struggles I was having with my faith."

"Yes," said Kaupon. "And where is your faith now?"

Jameson stared into the fire. "I'm not sure," he said. "As of late, I have many questions. It's as if I have opened up to a whole new world. I feel like I am about to reach a new level of understanding."

"Good," said Kaupon. "You are correct about this transition you are going through. Keep your faith strong and your mind open and you will come through this just fine."

"That's reassuring," said Jameson. "Do you have any other advice?"

"Do you still practice the Violet Flame of St. Germane?" asked Kaupon.

"Yes," said Jameson. "Of course."

"Show me," said Kaupon. "Calm your thinking and stare into the fire."

Jameson did as he was told.

"Now, I want you to imagine that the flame is the color of violet. The highest frequency color you can imagine."

Jameson stared at the flame, at first imagining the absence of the red and yellow hues in the fire. He tried to visualize a blue flame, hot and pure in it's essence. To his surprise, the fire matched what he saw in his mind's eye.

"Yes," said Kaupon. "Now, higher, brighter. Think about the top of the rainbow. Think of pure violet light."

Jameson focused. The fire glowed purple, then bright indigo.

"Yes," said Kaupon. "Good."

"What is the purpose of this exercise, Father?" asked Jameson.

"Indulge me for a moment." The fire flickered. "Concentrate on the violet flame."

Jameson turned his full attention to the fire. Soon, a deep violet color dominated the flames. After a moment or two, he felt something different. Whereas before it provided heat and health, it now gave him peace and wisdom.

"You have been practicing meditation, opening your mind to new things," said Kaupon. "I want you to meditate and bring the violet flame into your heart."

Jameson closed his eyes. With his eyes closed, he did not see the flame jump from the fireplace into his heart, but he felt it. He was now the source of heat and health, of life and wisdom. The flame burned throughout his body, transmuting his flesh into something greater, something he could only define as vitality. He took a deep breath, and another new experience came upon him. Like oxygen on a fire, the prana he breathed stoked the fire of his heart, adding a new dimension to what he could best define as love.

"It's Christ Consciousness," said Kaupon. "Pure and simple."

For the first time in his life, Jameson felt like he had found the answer to his life long quest, even to the secrets of nature and the universe. In that moment and in that chair, he was eternal, at peace with himself and everything around him. He had only mankind's highest interest at heart, seeing humans as children kept in a crowded and hectic nursery called Earth.

"It is especially important now that you practice this exercise," said Kaupon. "You have been meditating, opening up the doors to your psychic awareness."

"Yes," said Jameson. "I have been having strange experiences as of late. I sometimes think I hear voices. I am especially sensitive and feel things differently. Do you know what I mean, Father?"

"I do," said Kaupon. "We all have an inner voice that speaks to us, but there are times we correctly identify that as a voice that comes from somewhere else. We can even have a conversation with this outer voice. There are even times when that conversation happens without our conscious knowledge."

"How is that possible?"

"We exist on many levels, in many different bodies. Just because we don't perceive them, does not mean they don't exist. And yet, if you try, you can perceive them, you can become consciously aware of these things. But I must warn you, not everything in this unperceived realm is benevolent. Like life on Earth, you can encounter the occasional thug, trickster, and scalawag. Rascals and scoundrels abound, so I tell you to avoid the places they congregate."

"How will I know these places?"

"You must trust your feelings and your instincts," said Kaupon. "You are learning to *see*. Right now, your vision is blurry, but it will improve. Have faith in yourself. Have faith in God. He has sent his angels to protect you."

Jameson smiled. "I met them earlier. They were here earlier."

Father Kaupon turned his head, looking behind the chair where Jameson was seated. "And they are still here now."

Jameson turned to see his guardian angel smiling, his hands resting gently on the back of the chair. Beside him were two other angels.

"Now that you are aware of them, you can call upon them and set them to task, just like you always have. You can ask for protection, guidance, healing, help, anything you need. Of course, there are things they cannot do, but you know these things. Angels are not in the business of wish fulfillment and don't ask them to pick winning lottery numbers for you."

Jameson laughed.

There was a burst of sound from outside the office.

"Ah, yes," said Kaupon. "Our time together draws to a conclusion. You must leave soon."

"Where should I go?" asked Jameson.

"Outside the door and to the left. There is a garden outside this building. Do you remember it?"

84

"Yes," said Jameson. "It is a peaceful place. I have often sat on the wooden benches there and contemplated life."

"Good," said Kaupon. "You will find your friend Cameron Singh there. You may not recognize him, but he will be the only one there by the time you find him. Like you, his time on Earth is not complete. He will be tempted to stay here, but you must bring him with you. Can you do that?"

"Yes, but where will I go from there?" asked Jameson.

"Back to Earth, of course," said Kaupon. "Unless you want to move on. I didn't mean to make your decision for you. I just assumed..."

"No, you are correct, Father," said Jameson. "I know my work on Earth is not yet done. I somehow know I am destined to live a long and full life."

There was a screech from the hallway, the sound of dolphin.

"Your friends will meet you after you find Singh," said Kaupon. "They will show you the way back. Just remember what I told you. Keep up with your spiritual practice, your prayers and meditation. If you hear a voice, question it. Ask *who are you*? *What do you want*? *Are you positive or negative energy, are you God or the Devil*? They must answer truthfully, your angels will see to that. Call upon them for protection and confirmation. Have faith in yourself as well as in God."

"That's a lot to do, Father Kaupon."

"And I'm sure you're up to the task," said Kaupon. "Look at you! A Cardinal."

There was another dolphin squeal from the hallway. Jameson turned towards the door, then back to Kaupon.

"Yes," said the Father. "You'd better go."

"Will I see you again?" asked Jameson.

"I live in your heart," he said. "You can see me as often as you like."

There was yet another call from the dolphin. Jameson got up and walked to the door. When he turned back to say goodbye, there was nothing. No fire, no desk, no office, no Father Kaupon. Only the door remained.

He closed his eyes for a moment and grasped the doorknob. He felt a reassuring hand on his shoulder as he twisted the knob.

Chapter 14
Man(n)y a Good Man Has Been Wrong

There was a fog, a dense condensate that clung to his skin like a too tight garment in the midst of a tropical heat wave. Manny pushed his way through it, not knowing where he was or where he was headed. He wasn't afraid of fog. To him, it was just a cloak made of moist, cold air, something that felt good to him. It was magical, a walk in the clouds.

It reminded him of many fog filled mornings he had spent walking to work.

The fog parted, and he found himself at the entrance to Manny's Beachside Bistro. Inside, a woman sat at a stool leaning against the bar. "About time you got here," she said. "I'm tired of self service. I need some personal service."

Manny instinctively went to the bar, standing opposite her on the other side of the counter. "What can I do for you?"

He looked into her eyes, deep pools of blue that he immediately fell into. She was not only beautiful, but positively stunning. Without a word, she leaned forward. Before he could react, her lips met his, wetting them with a warm, deep kiss.

There was no resistance. He returned the kiss, as passionately as he could imagine in his best fantasy of what a wet kiss should be.

"Now that's what I call service," she said, her hand pressed to the back of his head, refusing to let him stop for long.

He reached beside himself, pushing the "self service"

sign aside. "We won't be needing this," he said between breaths.

"Not if we want to dance." she said. She held out her hands, inviting him closer. Her touch held the promise of passion. Manny met her touch, electric current flowing through his body like lightning through a ground rod. He was suddenly beside her, the music hot and loud, a Latin beat that made his blood flow red and fast. It was as if the bar were immaterial, nonexistent and ethereal, he walked right through it and out onto the open floor. She was in his arms and they were spinning and dancing like they had been partners their whole life.

The music played on. He didn't know where it was coming from. He didn't care. He held her hand, expertly letting her twirl wildly about him. She was no amateur, and her movements were as fluid as anyone who studied and worked hard to reach such heights of grace.

Manny was not without his moves either. He played her partner well, following what he had learned in his dance training. His job was simple, and he accepted that he was little more than a frame for her art. He found it remarkable that he could read her next move and act in such close harmony with her.

"Where did you learn to dance like this?" he asked.

"I could ask you the same question," she said. "But does it really matter? We are dancing, after all."

"Yes," he said. "You're quite good, you know."

She smiled, spinning into a pirouette. "Thank you."

"Trained in ballet I see."

The music stopped and she drew closer. "That's not all I'm trained in."

She pushed him gently and he fell backwards, landing on a soft mattress.

"Where did that come from?" asked Manny.

"Does it matter?" she asked, poised to pounce on him like a hungry leopard.

"Whoa," said Manny. "I don't think I'm ready for this. We just met."

"Don't you believe in love at first sight?" she asked.

"Maybe I do, but I still like to take things easy."

"Oh, come now, Manny Dubois," she said, standing over him. "You can't fool me. I know exactly what you want."

"Maybe you know what you want, but you really don't know what I want," he said. "How could you?"

"That's not true," she said. "I'm the perfect partner for you. I know exactly what you want."

"How could you? We just met. You don't even know me."

She laughed at his naivety. "You're a shy boy, even though you don't show it," she said. "You like it when the women take the offensive and chase you. You like to flirt and tease, but when it comes down to it, you're looking for a wedding partner. Now, why do you want to get married so bad, Manny?"

"You tell me, you know so much," said Manny.

"You're first marriage was a disaster, so much so that it ended in a horrible divorce," she said. "You ran away to the Eighth Day Village of the Sun, taking the community job of running the Beachside Bistro for the locals and tourists. You were like a wounded animal, hiding your weakness behind a protective wall of personality."

"How do you know these things?"

"Easy, because I am you."

Manny felt his jaw drop a few inches.

"Don't be so surprised," she said. "Anything is possible in the Point of Departure."

"I still don't get it," he said. "How can you be me?"

"I came from deep inside you," she said. "I am a part of you. I represent what you imagine to be your perfect woman."

"How is this possible?"

"I told you, anything is possible in the Point of Departure," she said. "The only limits are the limits of your imagination. Face the truth, Manny. I am the woman you have been searching for. Stay here with me. We can have a good life together. I will make you happy."

She fell onto the mattress beside him. Like Pygmalion, his dream had come to life, but something felt off. She went to kiss him but he avoided her, turning his head like a reluctant schoolboy afraid of getting cooties.

"What's the matter?" she asked, sensing his apprehension. She backed away and stood up, looking down at him on the bed, waiting for an answer. "Well?"

He searched his thoughts for a moment before choosing his words carefully. "You're not real," he said.

"Neither is the woman you're searching for," she said.

"Now, that's not true," he said.

"You're wrong," she said. "You have projected the image of me onto every woman you have been with, Manny. I even carry the emotional weight of your bartender syndrome."

"Bartender syndrome?" he asked. "What's that?"

"You know it well. You named it," she said. "It's that little bit of doubt your harbor about sleeping with a woman. You tell yourself everyone wants to sleep with the bartender, but nobody wants to marry him."

"Caroline was not like that," he said.

"Face it, Manny, Caroline is not coming back," she said. "You're stuck with me. She left because you tried to project this image of me onto her. You have been in love with me all along, Manny Dubois. Not a real woman, but a fantasy you created."

Was it the truth that stung? It was not as if he did not desire her. She was his dream girl, perfect for him in ways he had yet to discover. Still, there was a nagging thought and the perception that this was not real. He might as well be talking to himself, and if she was right about her origin and identity, he was doing just that.

She continued to look down at him, a gaze that held him captive for the moment. Her movements were slow and seductive. She shimmered for a second, and when she became focused again, she was wearing lingerie and bedtime attire.

"I'm demi-sexual," he said, trying to slow her down. "I need a strong feeling before I jump into bed with someone."

"Then feel this," she said.

She jumped, leaping into the air to land on top of him. He braced himself, his hands up to absorb the shock. Instead, she fell into him. Like a ghost, she passed through his hands and into his body. He felt a rush of energy, something beyond any sexual ecstasy he had ever felt.

With each wave of passion came understanding and self-knowledge. He felt her deep inside him, inside his thoughts. He knew the truth in her words, they were his own after all.

There are times we hide things from ourselves, for whatever reason, and it distorts our self image. This appeared to be the case with Manny. When he looked beyond the facade of his fantasy, he saw his search for true love as a way to distract himself from the real task that was at hand.

The image he created was not the real Manny Dubois,

merely a projected form of his ego. It was just as unreal as the dream girl he had been talking to.

She was inside him now, tucked safely away in his imagination. Through some kind of magic, he had been exposed to his inner thoughts in a way that allowed him to map his desires and see the landscape of his inner life. In that brief moment of realization, Manny Dubois understood that the greatest task that stands before every person on the Earth is to know and conquer themselves. Now that these things had surfaced, it would be hard to hide them again. Best to confront them and deal with them.

He laid there thinking, these thoughts churning like froth in a turbid sea.

There was a high pitched squeal, the sound of dolphin calling.

And just like that, the area around him became an ocean. The mattress disappeared. He fell down into it, plunging deep until he bobbed back up to the surface.

There was another high pitched squeal as a dolphin broke through water beside him. Beneath the waves, he opened his eyes. There was Barnheart, his hand on the fin of Neptune. He felt a thump. Valencia tapped him gently, squealing and nodding her head.

The Professor waved to him with his free hand, motioning him to follow. He spoke, something Manny did not think possible underwater. "We're getting out of here, going back to where we belong, back to New Maya City of Worlds. You can come with us, or you can stay here until you decide to depart for somewhere else."

He thought about the imaginary girlfriend he carried inside him somewhere, a projection of his self. He thought of this place, how it shifted with his thoughts to create whatever he imagined. "It would be little more than being trapped in a dream," he said.

92

"Ah," said Barnheart. "But life is but a dream as well."

"Come dream with us," said Valencia.

With determination, Manny reached out and grabbed on to her. She squealed in delight and took off swimming, following Amanhatayotep and Barnheart as they raced through the water. He tightened his grip, holding on to her like his life depended on it.

Chapter 15
Blueprint for a Temple

Yorgi and Petra found themselves on a smooth, grassy plain. A forest of green grew nearby. Next to them was a wall of stone. The rock in it was fitted together as tight as any laser cut jigsaw puzzle.

"I recognize this wall," said Yorgi. "I know this place."

"You mean, this time, not this place," said Petra. "Everything looks clean and fresh and new."

"Yes. You're right," said Yorgi. "I see it now. I know the place and the time as well."

"So do I," said Petra. "We are in New Maya City of Worlds."

"Long before the modern city was built," said Yorgi.

"Yes," said Petra. "Even before the first city was here."

"Before the ancient temple too," said Yorgi. "No sign of ruins"

"Or construction."

Everything was still and quiet, as if someone had put a video on pause. There were some stone houses and grass shacks in the distance, but no humans. Birds hung lifeless in mid air. A jaguar sat motionless on a rock. Then, without warning, the world sprang into action around them. They watched quietly as stone after stone rose from somewhere behind the wall, floating in the air until it landed gently nearby.

"Look," said Yorgi. "We are right. The stones are forming the foundation of what looks like the modern remains of the temple."

Petra looked around. "I don't see anyone else here.

94

Are we moving the stones?"

"No," said Yorgi. "We've seen something like this before in our dreams. The temple at Uxmal was built this way."

"Yes," she said. "The legend says Uxmal was built in a day using magic like this. Of course, we know it wasn't magic, just some special abilities."

"I didn't know the temple at New Maya City of Worlds was also built this way," said Yorgi. "For some reason we are being shown how it was constructed."

"Is this a dream?" she asked.

"It could be," said Yorgi. "Or it could be a vision from the past."

"Or even the future," she said. "I can faintly see New Maya City of Worlds surrounding us." When Yorgi scanned, he saw it too, the city appearing in the otherwise empty surroundings like a hologram, both real and imaginary.

"Perhaps it is something like that," he said. "Let's continue watching for now. I feel like there is something here for us to learn."

Large, heavy stones continued to move, an aerial parade of rock that ended with each piece of the temple falling into place.

It continued, walls rising, inner rooms forming, stairs ascending.

"It's definitely the temple," said Petra.

"Yes," said Yorgi. "This must be how it was made."

"But it was never complete," said Petra.

"It was complete, just fallen into ruins," said Yorgi.

"You're right," said Petra. "Pieces of it were just missing."

"The archaeologists asked for our help," said Yorgi. "They brought us here shortly after we moved to the Eighth Day Village of the Sun."

"I remember," said Petra. "They wanted us to reconstruct the temple but we couldn't. There was no magic here, at least I didn't feel it. Most of the stones that once formed the temple are gone. There was really nothing to rebuild or excavate, just a pile of old ruins."

"Yes," said Yorgi. "How does rock disappear?"

"Maybe the same way people disappear," said Petra.

"Maybe," said Yorgi. "That, or people take them for other purposes. Someone could have used the stone to build something else."

"The adults dug and searched and found nothing."

"That's not true," said Yorgi. "Some stones were found in the forest, the roots of trees wrapped around them. Some were even buried, discovered only by accident when new activity disturbed the ground."

"How do you know that?" asked Petra.

Yorgi looked at her. "Don't you remember? The archaeologists of New Maya told us that."

"Oh," said Petra. "Look! Pay attention. There's a giant crystal coming this way."

The crystal floated above them, draped in cloth but visible from the ground. It moved over the walls of the temple, descending through the unfinished, open roof into the center of the construct. Stones quickly fell into place above it as the temple continued to form.

When it was completed it was unlike anything they had seen. Similar to many of the temples in the area, it was tall with a steep set of stairs leading to the top. Off to one side there was an entrance at ground level, a lintel of carved stone over a corridor of darkness. The temple itself was built to accurately line up with features on the Earth as well as the heavens. Window openings were precise and measured. A tall, wooden observation tower stood beside it, a place to view the sky and mark the progress of the planets and stars. In a final act, writing appeared on the walls both inside and outside the temple.

"I remember studying the ruins, but I would never have guessed that the final temple looked like this," said Yorgi.

"Are we dreaming?" asked Petra. "Because if we are, then this is just a fantasy."

"How can it be?" asked Yorgi. "We are both having the same dream."

"How do I know you are not just a part of my dream?" asked Petra.

Yorgi laughed. "Because that would make you just a part of my dream, and we both know that's not true. Besides..." He reached out and pinched her and she let out a squeal that quickly became laughter.

They went back to looking at the temple. "We could never build something this grand," said Petra.

"Yes, we could," said Yorgi. "Let's go take a closer look. We can study it up close. That way when we get back, we can put it together just like it is here. The archaeologists would probably like that."

"Okay," said Petra. "It would be kinda fun. Do you think they'd let us make something like this?"

"Does it matter right now?" said Yorgi. "Come on, let's have a closer look and see what we can learn."

The ground level corridor looked dark and ominous. "It's blocked by a stone," said Petra. "But there is another entrance on the top."

With that, they began to explore, climbing all the way to the top, then descending into the structure to research the intricate design and the functional purpose of the sacred space within. A strange glow kept the passageways lit, and in some of the rooms there were fires burning in pits and on wall torches.

"The temple is empty. Who lit these fires?" asked Petra.

"We may never know," said Yorgi. "Then again, it could be magic, like Uxmal."

When they finished looking everywhere, they emerged exhausted. The sun began to set on the horizon, shadows reaching long and dark across the smooth plain of grass. The temple seemed to glow in the fading light, inlays of gold and precious stones reflecting bright and sparkling in the amber rays of sunset.

"That's something I haven't noticed before," said Yorgi. "Look how the rocks sparkle."

Petra moved closer to study it. "There are precious gems and crystals embedded in the rock," she said. She put her hand against the rock and laughed.

"What is it?" asked Yorgi.

"He just told me where we could find more rocks like him," she said. "He's a very wise rock, one with the Eternal."

"That's good," said Yorgi. "I hate stupid rocks."

"He says this is real and not a dream," she said. "The spirits of many stones have come together to create this vision for us."

"What else does he say?" asked Yorgi.

"It's sad. He has predicted his future. He knows he will be old and no longer at the temple when we leave the Point of Departure. It's why we have never met, why he is not at the temple in our present time. Painfully, he will be chipped away, piece by piece, the gems that are part of his life stolen and traded for a small amounts of wealth. The fools that do this have no idea of the true value of this rock. But, as the precious stones are his children, through

98

them he will travel and see much of the world. It is his destiny, and it will increase his knowledge and understanding of humanity."

"I see," said Yorgi.

"He is sad because he will never be whole again," said Petra. "I wonder if that is what Divine Source feels like, separated into a billion zillion things."

"If God or Divine Source wanted to be whole, all It would have to do is make time run backwards."

"That would make the rock whole, too."

"Ask the rock if he knows anything about the great crystal that lives at the core of the temple."

Petra put her hand to the rock. "He says to be cautious of it. It can open the doorway to the Point of Departure. Many go but few return, he says."

"Then we must be careful," said Yorgi.

"The design of the temple holds the energy of the crystal," said Petra. "The crystal must not be exposed to the sunlight. To do so is disaster."

"That explains a lot," said Yorgi.

"Maybe it explains how all the people in New Maya disappeared," said Petra.

"Maybe it even explains where we are now," said Yorgi sadly. "Thank him."

"I already have," said Petra. She pat the stone gently, rubbing it as if it were her pet.

The sun dipped below the horizon, shadows merging with the darkness. A canopy of stars shined in the sky. The twins grew tired. They laid down on the grassy meadow, but the stone told them to go inside the temple where they would be safe.

A meteor lit the heavens, a falling star.

"Let's make a wish," said Petra.

"I wish we knew the way home," said Yorgi.

"You're not supposed to tell your wish," said Petra. "Now it won't come true."

"Then I'm glad you kept your wish a secret."

As Petra fell into a slumber that night, she wondered about something. If she made the same wish as Yorgi, would it still come true? Then again, her wish was slightly different. She didn't wish that they knew the way home, she wished instead that they were home."

Chapter 16
Don't Forget the Reincarnated Atlantean

Cardinal Jameson stepped through the doorway. Despite the room disappearing behind him, the corridor was the same as he remembered it. He followed it to the left and down a staircase. It was a short walk from there to the garden.

It was secluded, walled off from the world that surrounded it. The park was large enough to accommodate many people, with benches and hammocks placed far enough apart to offer plenty of privacy. There were ponds scattered about, places of quiet reflection. Thick foliage and dense walls absorbed any stray sounds that drifted in from beyond.

Jameson kept a quick pace. Father Kaupon had imparted a sense of urgency about the situation. He didn't want to disturb the tranquility of the park by calling out for his friend's name, but the idea began to appeal to him. Moving up and down paths, it seemed that everywhere he checked, there were no people. Odd because this was a popular park.

He darted down yet another path, coming at the end to a small grotto bounded by tall rocks on one side and a line of flowering azaleas on the other. He climbed up on top of the rock, above the height of the trees, and he looked out hoping to spy some sign of Cameron Singh.

He remembered what Father Kaupon had told him and he spoke out loud, calling for assistance. "All right, my angel friends. I need your help. Fly high on your wings and scour the park. See if you can find any signs of my friend."

Jameson imagined the angels helping him. In his

mind, he saw them flying high over the landscape, looking down on the land. He closed his eyes for a moment, thinking about what it would be like to fly with them. He felt at ease, the tension that had dominated his earnest search of the park dripped off his body like the remains of a warm afternoon rain.

When he opened his eyes again, he saw a golden glow in the distance.

"Who else but Cameron Singh could produce such a Light," he said. Looking left and right, he got his bearings and headed for the source. Following the main promenade, he reached the trailhead to the path that led towards the golden glow. It went upward, over rocks and tree roots, a narrow path that finally opened up into a flat, grassy setting. There was a lotus pond to one side, a spray of water trickling into a shallow pool. Carefully planted flower gardens, their edges straight and true, their contents lush and plenty, lined the far edges. Trees abounded, cherry trees, fruit trees, fragrant pines and weepy willows.

Scanning the area, there was only one person on the plateau, seated at a wooden bench near the lotus pond. There was an empty bench across from them. By some trick of his eye, he thought he caught a glimpse of a fading golden glow on that bench. It could easily be a sparkle of sunlight reflecting from somewhere. There were wind chimes and crystals hanging from tree branches, a number of things that could catch the light. Then again, he thought, maybe it was the source of the glow that guided him here.

The person seated on the other bench was certainly not glowing. He approached carefully, knowing what it is like to be disturbed so suddenly when meditating in a peaceful place like this. When he got close and in earshot, he quietly called, "Cameron Singh?"

The person on the bench turned, a beautiful woman,

attractive beyond belief. She had to be the mold God used to create the angels. All that were missing were her wings.

She looked familiar. Beneath her gentle features, he thought he recognized her. A past parishioner perhaps? Maybe someone he knew from school. So familiar. "Excuse me," he said.

"I heard you Cardinal Jameson," she said. Slowly she stood up, turning to face him. She was clad in some kind of primitive priestess garb, ornate and ceremonial. It did nothing to hide her body. Her skin appeared golden, or perhaps tanned to perfection. Her garments were low cut, exposing things the Cardinal would rather not see. From beneath the folds in her skirt, her long legs peeked through slits as she turned to face him.

It was then she spoke again, and he knew the truth. "Yes, Cardinal Jameson. It's me. Your friend, Cameron Singh."

"Father Kaupon said I might not recognize you when I found you," said Jameson.

Singh looked down at herself, twisting in a feminine gesture, her skirt flowing about her hips as it floated above the ground. Her cloak fell open and Jameson glimpsed at how she was scantily clad beneath it, voluptuous breasts held tight in an ornately decorated leather and gold bra. Her short overskirt was decorated with precious gems and hung below an expanse of naked belly flesh. There were numerous piercings and tattoos visible, sacred markings and rites of passage.

"Is this you in another incarnation?" he asked.

"You might say that," said Singh. "But, actually, this is me in my present incarnation."

"How..." said the Cardinal, but he did not have time to voice his question.

There was a splash from the lotus pond. They both

looked over. A dolphin was sticking his head out of the water, his flippers fluttering to catch their attention.

"Yes," said Singh. "Now that you are here, it's time for us to leave."

"I would like nothing better than to depart the Point of Departure," said Jameson. "Do you know where we need to go to get out of here?"

"I don't," said Singh, pointing to the dolphin. "But I'm sure he does."

The dolphin shook his head in a yes motion. He dove beneath the surface of the pond.

Jameson walked over and stared down into the water. "It's shallow," he said. He turned towards Singh. "How does he do that?"

Cameron shrugged.

Without warning, the surface of the water erupted and the dolphin shot up into the air. Instead of falling back into the pond, he was suspended, floating as easily as he would in the open sea.

In a plain voice, he said to them, "Well, what are you waiting for? Grab my fin and I'll take us out of here."

His voice sounded familiar and they trusted the dolphin. Reaching up, Jameson latched on to the fin. He reached his hand out for Cameron, his grip tight and secure. The dolphin took off in a lurch, his powerful caudal fin swatting the air like it was water.

Chapter 17
The Rescue

The sun rose again, and although they were still on a smooth, grassy plain, it was a different place. Yorgi and Petra awoke to find the temple was gone, bits of it remaining, present only as decaying ruins. They woke up between the broken stones and the tools left behind by archaeologists and scientists. New Maya City of Worlds stood proudly around it, a respectable distance away, daring not to intrude on the slumber of the ancients. Nearby, trenches had been dug, deep and wide, a big square that connected on all sides, the remains of Doctor Candle's work to excavate the crystal.

The City was still empty. In the distance, a crashed and broken crystal airship lay in ruins.

"Was it all just a dream?" asked Petra.

"Maybe," said Yorgi. "I'm not too sure."

"Are we really here?" she asked.

Yorgi reached out to pinch her. When she figured out what he was going to do, she moved back and laughed. "You know, it's pointless to do that. It still hurts where you did it in Point of Departure."

"Either way, it looks like we are back in our world," said Yorgi.

"What about the others?" asked Petra.

"Maybe they are around here somewhere," said Yorgi. The twins scanned the area.

"They may be injured in that airship crash," said Petra. Her voice suddenly dropped. "Were we in an accident? I don't remember."

"It doesn't matter," said Yorgi. "Let's go over there to check first."

A quick search revealed nothing.

"There's no one here," said Yorgi. "The whole city is still empty. It's just us."

"Which makes me think, where are we? In the dream world, the Point of Departure, our world, or even some kind of weird pocket universe?"

"Does it matter?" said Yorgi. "Here is where we are."

"Okay. So, what do you want to do?" asked Petra.

"Let's practice building the temple like we said we would," said Yorgi. "Don't you think it would be fun?"

"Yes!" she answered. "While it's fresh in our memory."

They walked back to the temple ruins and surveyed the site. The Ascension Crystal lay askew in the center of it all. The wind had blown a blanket over it, partially hiding it from the sun. Around it lay a mess left by the curious minds that had unearthed the stone and opened the doorway to the Point of Departure.

Yorgi studied what was left. "We're going to need more rock," he said.

"I'll go look where the jewel rock told me I could find more of his clan," said Petra. "He said they would volunteer to come here if we asked politely."

"Great," said Yorgi. "I'm going to do what I can here, maybe move some rocks and see if I can at least get the crystal upright and covered up."

Within the Point of Departure Amanhatayotep and Valencia swam with all their strength, Barnheart and Manny in tow. Their fins ached with the effort. The sea they swam in was dense and movement was difficult despite how much effort they put out. Then there was the

106

strange sensation of breathing without breathing. Unlike an earthbound sea where they would surface occasionally to breathe, this realm had no surface, no air to breathe.

Manny struggled with similar issues. He couldn't get over the idea that he was, to his perception, underwater and yet able to talk. He and Barnheart were carrying on a conversation, shouting at times to hear each other over the gurgling torrent of fluid that rushed past their ears.

"Where do you think they are taking us?" asked Manny.

"Back to our world," said Valencia.

Another thing he couldn't get over. The dolphin could also talk.

"I thought you said you didn't want to stay here," she said.

"I wasn't sure," said Manny. "I had an offer I was considering."

She let out a squeal, dolphin noise that Manny interpreted as something between surprise and laughter.

"She's right," said Barnheart. "You could stay here, but sooner or later you would have to depart."

"For where?" asked Manny,

"Somewhere else, I guess," said Barnheart. "You can't stay in one place forever."

"Why not?" asked Manny.

"You should know that better than anybody," said Barnheart. "You're a physicist. You know that energy continually exchanges between potential and kinetic. And, not to make a pun, you have more potential than this, my boy."

"What about the rest of our group?" asked Manny. "Have you seen the twins or the Cardinal?"

"The twins have already departed," said Barnheart. "At

least, that's what Amanhatayotep told me. They're waiting for us back in the City."

"They wait for us to return," said Amanhatayotep.

"What about Barclay and the Cardinal?" asked Manny.

"We will rendezvous with them both shortly when we near the barrier," said Amanhatayotep.

"There is still the matter of the correct exit point, from what I understand," said Barnheart, explaining things to Manny. "The Point of Departure has an infinite number of destinations possible when anyone leaves. You see the importance of finding the correct exit point."

They heard dolphin squeals in the distance.

"It appears Barclay has found it," said Valencia.

"That's the signal," said Amanhatayotep.

The pace quickened. The two dolphin did not think they could swim any faster, especially with humans in tow, but the mind can overcome such weaknesses at times, especially when called to task.

Manny sensed something beside him and turned to see a third dolphin, this one hauling two humans. "Cardinal Jameson!" he called out. "Who is that with you?"

"I found Cameron Singh," he said. "She's here with me."

Manny looked at the woman. He didn't quite process the Cardinal's use of the pronoun, referring to her as Cameron Singh. He didn't have time to think about it.

Jameson gripped Singh tightly as the dolphin accelerated, pulling ahead of Valencia and Amanhatayotep. "Follow me!" shouted the dolphin.

The pair began to work even harder, trying to keep up with the lead dolphin. He was strong, towing two humans at once. The fluid felt like gelatin at times, straining all their muscles. The added weight of Manny and Barnheart was a burden of stone for Amanhatayotep and Valencia. It was not easy to drag them about. Humans are not as streamlined as dolphin.

"Faster!" shouted the lead dolphin. "The exit point is right ahead. It must be met with force. Faster!"

"What is it?" asked Manny. "I don't understand."

"Hang tight everyone," said the lead dolphin. "Whatever it is, we're about to hit it."

There was a sound, like cracking glass, or more accurately, like a crystal shattering. A bright light blinded them all just seconds before they lost consciousness.

Chapter 18
Do We Have Insurance?

Manny shook himself awake. His thoughts were cloudy and his body ached, but he felt alive again. Standing up. He rubbed his shoulder trying to remember where he got the pain he was feeling.

"What happened?" he asked himself.

The wreckage was nearby. The crystal airship lay in pieces, broken remnants of debris massed like so much garbage left at the curb on collection day. He rubbed the back of his head, cobwebs still blocking the experience from his memory. Like waking from a dream, there were bits and fragments to build on, but not quite a full picture. The missing fragments ached in his consciousness like a lost limb amputated at a battlefield hospital.

He heard a squeal nearby, the sound of a dolphin.

"Of course, the dolphin!" he said, another piece of the puzzle falling into place, but all he could remember was something about a dolphin, nothing more. He looked around for the source of the sound.

He heard a weak voice from the wreckage. "Help me."

He recognized the voice. "Barclay?" he called, but there was no answer.

Manny stepped over a broken mound of crystal that looked like a pile of winter icicles. He pushed away what remained of the broken bay door. The passenger compartment was in shambles, seats lying askew, the supplies scattered everywhere. The tank of water appeared intact. There was a splash and he saw a shadow move inside it. "Dolphin," he said, sounding like a preschooler seeing one for the first time. He stared for a minute, watching it move around. "Of course," he said, the sight of it beginning to confirm and support fragments of memory.

He heard a groan from the corner. He saw a hand sticking out between a roll of emergency netting and a Geiger counter. He made his way to it, pushing through the layer of provisions, camping supplies, and instruments that littered the floor. He dug away at everything he could, starting near the hand. Soon he had an arm and a face exposed.

"Barnheart," he said. "Are you okay, Professor?"

"Manfred," he said, his voice groggy and distant.

"Let me get you out of there, Professor," he said. He began digging as best he could, moving heavy objects aside using a support pole as a lever. "There don't seem to be any broken bones," he said as more of the body was exposed. "How do you feel?"

"Okay," said Barnheart. "What happened?"

"I'm not sure," said Manny. "It appears we were in an accident."

"Yes," said Barnheart. "We hit a barrier of some kind." The Professor scanned the area. "What about the twins?"

"I don't know," said Manny. "You're the first one I've found. Here, let me help you stand up and we'll get you outside."

With effort they were soon on the lawn. Manny found some camping gear and chairs, making them comfortable. Barnheart breathed easy, inspecting himself for damage.

"You have a couple of bruises," said Manny. "But other than that you look okay. I've got a first aid kit over here. Let me treat some of those wounds."

Barnheart looked back towards the ship. "Where is the Cardinal?"

"I'm here," said Jameson. He emerged from behind the wreckage. "I don't know how, but I got thrown clear when we crashed. I landed on a pile of straw in a field over there."

"Are you okay?" asked Manny.

"Fine, fine," he said, patting his sides.

There was another weak cry from the wreckage.

"Barclay," said Manny. "I forgot about him." He passed the first aid kit to the Cardinal who took up the task of helping the Professor.

"Look," said Barnheart pointing towards the temple. "The Gorgofsky Twins."

Manny turned and looked before moving off. He thought he saw rock floating in the air but he thought better of it.

"We'll go check on them in a while," said the Cardinal. "After I finish bandaging you up."

Manny worked his way back inside the broken airship, this time clearing a path through the mess of supplies to the cockpit. The door was jammed and he had to move debris away from around the base. Using his lever he was finally able to pry the door open.

Inside was a dolphin lying on its side. It looked helpless and wounded, a shard of crystal embedded in its side. "Help," it said, the words coming out dry and empty.

Manny moved beside the fallen mammal. The ship was tilted an an angle, the tail of the dolphin pointed down. He pushed gently against it, realizing it weighed much more than he could move, even in a fireman's carry, if that was possible.

He went back into the wrecked passenger cabin, sifting through the supplies and searching for something. When he found it, he returned to the cockpit. Using a sharp knife, a pair of pliers, and a gentle touch, he carefully removed the crystal embedded in the dolphin's side. He dabbed that with a towel and used duct tape to seal the wound. "I can't do much more than that for now," said Manny. "But I'll find a way to get you to one of our veterinarians at the Eighth Day Village of the Sun."

"Water," said the dolphin, the voice as weak as a desert wind through a cactus.

Manny brushed it aside, but he noted that it was the second time the dolphin had spoken.

"You need a drink of water?" asked Manny, but then looking down at the dolphin he realized what the animal meant. His skin was dry and mottled. "Oh," he said. "You need water to live in."

Manny again began to think about how he could lift a heavy animal and transport it to water. It was obvious that it was suffering. Then he had another thought. If this dolphin was here, and the other one in the tank, then where was Barclay McKenner? Maybe his friend was underneath the dolphin, buried in cockpit debris and broken crystal.

"Cardinal Jameson, Professor Barnheart," he called. "Can you please come and help?" He heard them pushing their way through the debris in the cockpit much as he had to.

"Oh my god," said Jameson, making the sign of the cross as he looked down at the dolphin.

"We need to get him back into the water," said Manny. "I can't do it alone."

Barnheart pulled a blanket from the debris in the passenger cabin. "The three of us should be able to move him with this."

Working together, they managed to roll the dolphin onto the blanket and move him out of the cockpit and into the passenger cabin. They did not find Barclay McKenner underneath him. The back of the crystal ship was intact, the tank of water was at an angle, but it was not cracked and it still held plenty of liquid.

"We need to get him in there," said Barnheart.

Stumbling over the debris again, they worked their way toward the water tank. There were squeals coming from it, cheers of support. The three men were finally able to lift the mammal to shoulder height and drop it gently into the tank.

The dolphin floated listless, acclimating to the conditions of the tank. The water felt good, natural around his skin. The duct tape held. His side was sore, but he knew it would heal and that he would be okay. He nodded, trying not to use the muscles around the wound.

It was the Professor who noticed it first. "There's three of them," he said.

"What?" said Manny, realizing the truth. "Where did the third one come from?"

He went back to the cockpit searching again for Barclay McKenner, calling for him. "Barclay!" he yelled, pushing his way through the debris. "Barclay!" Searching, he found nothing.

The back of his mind let loose another secret. *The Point of Departure,* he thought. They were words he didn't understand and he said them over and over until something clicked. *I remember not one but three dolphins, or was it two?* His mind began working like a tiller attached to a tractor, exposing fresh dirt and rocks from the dark, hidden places where they were buried. And just as sudden, he stumbled upon a cemetery of memories, thoughts and experiences entombed and still trapped with his mind, in the Point of Departure.

He was interrupted. "Come quickly," called Professor Barnheart. He was next to the tank of dolphin. "As you were shouting for your friend, the wounded dolphin in the tank acknowledged your calls."

The dolphin stuck its head above water. In a high, squeaky voice it said, "It's me, Manny."

It didn't process, but a slow, nagging thought entered Manny's mind. "Could it be Barclay McKenner?"

The Professor was at his side. "I'm not sure," he said. "Are we still, perhaps, in some kind of dream world?"

"He spoke to me," said Manny. "I was sure I heard his voice."

"I heard it too," said Barnheart. "You were not imagining it."

"How could this happen?" asked the Cardinal.

There was a voice from behind them. "Oh, believe me. It could happen."

They turned to see a woman at the edge of the wreckage. "I'm sorry you broke your airship. Is there anything I can do to help?"

"And who are you?" asked Barnheart.

Before an answer could come, Cardinal Jameson let out a sigh and a nod. "Cameron Singh," said the holy man. "So it wasn't a dream." He turned towards Singh. "I'm so glad to see you again, With you here now, my friend, we are all accounted for." He said a brief silent prayer of thanks.

"Cameron Singh?" said Manny in surprise.

"Yes, Manny," said the woman. "It's me. Unlike Barclay McKenner, at least I retained human form."

"But a woman?" said Manny.

"Does it matter?" said Singh, a hint of anger in her voice. "I am human at least. You should all feel lucky that you didn't change into something and lose your self in the Point of Departure."

A hoarse voice came from the tank. "Maybe not lose your self, but find your true self," said Barclay McKenner. "It seems we have both been repurposed."

Manny shook his head.

Barnheart laughed, then turned serious as he surveyed the wreckage. "I hope we had insurance," he said.

"One thing we don't have anymore is a pilot," said Manny. "I don't know how we're going to get everyone out of here and back, but I'll do my best."

The dolphin became agitated.

"Don't worry," said Manny, answering their unspoken concerns. "I'll walk back to the Village if need be."

"I think they are trying to tell you that Barclay is still a pilot," said Barnheart.

Manny shook his head.

"I'm sure there are airships in the village that we can use," suggested Singh.

"Before I do that, I want to at least assess the damage to this airship," said Manny.

"Okay," said Barnheart. "While you do that, I'll go check on the twins. They are in my care after all."

"I'd like to go with you," said the Cardinal.

"Go ahead," said Singh. "Manny and I will join you shortly."

Chapter 19
Construction Crew

Barnheart limped, the pain and bruises in his side making him move slowly.

"You had the strength to help us move the dolphin," said the Cardinal. "But I'm afraid you over exerted yourself, my friend."

"I'm inclined to agree," said Barnheart.

"My old football coach would tell you to walk it off," said Jameson.

"It's not as bad as it looks," said the Professor.

"Still, I hear you grunting with the effort," said Jameson.

"It's called getting older, Cardinal," said Barnheart. "I normally sound like this on a bad day."

As the two men neared the temple they saw the children hard at work. Stones levitated in the air, pieces of them falling off like dust as Petra shaped them. From there they moved into place like obedient soldiers, lining up where Yorgi made them feel comfortable, forming a new community of stone.

Barnheart and the Cardinal watched with interest and awe.

"I've never seen anything like this," said the Cardinal.

"Remarkable, isn't it," said Barnheart.

"A tribute to the power we all have within us," said the Cardinal. "I would not have believed it had I not seen it with my own eyes."

"I thought you were a man of faith," said Barnheart. "Don't you people have a habit of believing in the unseen?"

"Just as scientists make a habit of having to prove everything," said Jameson.

Barnheart laughed.

"But things like this lie beyond my ken," said Jameson.

"And yet you accept it as truth?"

"How can I not? Not only do I see it, but I sense it as well. With all my being."

Barnheart continued to stare at the children working. "I know how you feel," he said. "It makes me think that, as humans, we have no limitations. All things are possible."

In the center of it all, the crystal righted itself, standing tall and firm as rock settled around it. Walls began to form, Yorgi carefully directing the rock while Petra continued to shape it. Soon, the crystal was enclosed, sunlight unable to touch it and activate it's power of ascension.

When they were finished, they turned and saw that they had an audience. "Professor Barnheart," yelled Petra. Together the twins ran towards him.

"I'm glad you're here," said Yorgi. "We were beginning to worry about you."

"Any longer and you would have been trapped between dimensions." said Petra.

"We fixed the crystal," said Yorgi, pointing to the work the twins were doing on the temple. "We learned how to do it in the Point of Departure. There's just a little bit more to do to finish up the temple around it."

"You're doing an excellent job!" said the Professor as he embraced them.

The twins smiled.

"We searched the wreckage of the airship earlier," said Yorgi.

"It was the first thing we did," said Petra. "There was no one there before."

"We only started to work on the temple out of boredom."

Petra turned to Yorgi. "We need to finish what we started," she said. "Otherwise the door to the Point of Departure may open again."

"Yes," said Yorgi.

"The Point of Departure," asked Barnheart. "Seems like I remember that term."

"No time now. If you can't remember, we'll explain it to you later," said Petra. "We have work to do."

The twins went back to the temple site a short distance away. The Cardinal and Barnheart found a shady spot where they laid down and watched them work. Like veterans returning home on a troop ship, they began to talk about their experiences. By sharing the trauma, it became more manageable. In the process, memories fell into place. Whether real or imagined, their minds constructed their own idea of what had happened. Such is the nature of memory.

Cameron Singh helped Manny empty the contents of the airship and assess the damage. "The power system is intact," he said. "I think it will fly with a little structural work."

"We can search for an aircar to borrow," said Singh. "There are plenty of abandoned ones in the City."

"It's the tank with the dolphin that I'm worried about," said Manny. "It's heavy, and I don't want to leave them behind if possible. Barclay needs medical attention." He put his hand against the tank. "I still can't believe he's a dolphin now."

"I'm finding it hard to believe I'm a woman," said Singh.

"It's going to take a period of adjustment for both of you," said Manny. "What about that other thing Barclay said."

"What do you mean?" asked Singh.

"The talk about losing something and finding your true self. Is this your true self, Cameron?"

Singh stopped working for a moment. "I don't know. Like you said, this will take some adjustment."

"The people around you, your old friends and your relatives, they'll have some adjusting to do, too" said Manny. "I noticed the Cardinal feels slightly uneasy around you."

"It's probably that old Catholic priest taboo against women," said Singh. "They're trained to keep their distance."

"Probably he has trouble dealing with you," said Manny. "You exude some kind of intense energy. I don't want to say it's sexual, but it is very enticing. You are a beautiful woman."

Singh blushed involuntarily, then gained control. "It's these clothes," said Singh. "I look like some kind of Hollywood actress wearing her costume in public. What is this get up?"

"You should know," said Manny. "You're still a reincarnated Atlantean with all your special abilities. Can't you ask your soul to explain it to you?"

"I guess I could," said Singh. "But I think I know the answer. Like Barclay said, we've been repurposed."

"And what is that purpose?" asked Manny.

"I'm not sure I know it, let alone understand it," said Singh.

"Why not go over there and meditate? Reactivate your Atlantean powers," he suggested. "I can handle this."

"Okay," she said. " I think I'll go down by the temple then. I'd like to meditate down there."

The twins were done with their work. It was a mighty temple, strong like a fortress, a solid structure. The pyramid design was captivating. A long, single flight of stairs ascended to the top, ending at a shaded observation deck of smooth stone. It was in every detail a copy of the one they had studied in the Point of Departure.

When they were finished, the twins just looked at each other and smiled. Barnheart called to them from under his shady tree. He had a backpack of drinks and supplies to share with them.

"Professor," they said excitedly. "Look at what we've done." Their voices were filled with the same glee children have when they want a parent to admire their accomplishments. Somehow, though, this was much more than a crayon drawing meant for the refrigerator door.

"Come on," said Yorgi. "Come see what we did."

Petra tugged at his arm. "Yes. Come, see."

"As soon as we eat," said Barnheart. "You must be hungry."

"Yes, we are," said Yorgi.

"I'm am hungry, too," said Petra.

The twins had been focused on their work. Now their focus slowly turned towards their bodies. Yorgi heard his stomach growl for attention. Petra made a simple observation. "We're hungry. That means we're not dreaming, doesn't it Professor?"

"Of course we're not dreaming," said Barnheart.

"And you've made such a beautiful thing here," said the Cardinal. "I'm still amazed at how you made it. To

121

witness it being constructed, with my own eyes. What a miracle."

Barnheart let out a sigh. "It makes you wonder, Your Eminence, how much more goes on in the world that we do not see."

Cameron Singh came walking across the meadow, on her way to meditation. She waved to them, then went back to admiring the temple. She moved to the base of the pyramid and started to ascend the stairs.

"She's a beautiful woman," said Barnheart. "I didn't know him, uh her, before this. I'd heard of Cameron Singh, but never had close contact or the opportunity to know him."

"I've learned a lot from him," said the Cardinal. "It's okay. I'm using the male pronoun because in my mind I'm talking about the old Cameron Singh. I won't have any trouble adapting or calling her she. It's strange, and I'm trying to not let this affect our friendship, but I know it will."

"What do you mean?" asked Petra. "She's still your friend, the same person you knew before. Just packaged differently."

"Just the same, she makes me feel … I don't know, different."

"Are you attracted to her?" asked Barnheart.

"Who wouldn't be?" said Jameson. "But I have taken a vow of chastity, and I have yet to break it. But, even if I were not a priest, I would remember that we are friends first and not take advantage of the situation"

"That's a noble thought, Father," said Barnheart. "But I'm sure your friend would not let that happen either."

"There are priests and men in the Vatican that would call this an abomination," said Jameson.

"Is that what you think it is?" asked Barnheart.

"I have more of an open mind," said Jameson. "And I have seen things today that are beyond anything I could ever imagine."

The twins became impatient again. "Enough talk," said Petra. "We've eaten already."

"Let's go to the temple now," said Yorgi.

"Yes," said the Cardinal "I want to look at it closely, too."

They helped Barnheart to his feet.

"Let's go inside," said Petra. "There's something we need to show you."

They led the men through the passageways and into the central chamber of the temple. A dim light entered the room through cleverly designed light tunnels. The center of the room was dominated by a giant crystal.

"I've never seen anything like that on my visits here," said Barnheart.

"What is it?" asked the Cardinal.

"The Ascension Crystal," said Petra. "And the cause of all this confusion."

"They unearthed it by accident," said Yorgi. "It was okay when it was buried in the ground."

"Or enclosed within the temple," said Petra.

"The direct sunlight activated it," said Yorgi. "They had no choice but to ascend. Everyone in New Maya ascended."

"The crystal did all this," said Barnheart. The thought of a crystal triggered something inside him. An image flashed in his head. He saw a man wearing a colored cloak over a simple tunic held in place with a belt decorated with hanging pouches. He had a long beard and a stiff gait. He was at a demonstration bench, not just any demonstration bench, but the one in his teaching laboratory. In his mind's eye, Barnheart watched the man open a jar of sulfur and put some on a glass plate. There was a crystal involved, not big like this one here. Smaller, shaped round like a lens, fitted into a stand. He watched the sulfur turn to gold in his vision. Then, in a moment's flash, that simple recollection grew to a memory of his whole experience, everything that had happened to him in the Point of Departure.

"Are you okay Professor?" asked Petra.

It took another second or two, but Barnheart answered her. "I remembered it. I remembered it all." He looked at the twins, then at the Cardinal.

"I suddenly remember what happened to me, too," said the Cardinal. "In vivid detail."

"Do you think the crystal has anything to do with that?" said Yorgi.

"Yes," said Petra. "Once we stood beside it, we remembered everything. Even how to build this temple."

"We traveled into the past and saw this temple being built for the first time," said Yorgi.

"It was easy to reconstruct it once we saw it being built," said Petra. "We think it was the same way the temple at Uxmal was built."

"Uxmal? You mean the legendary temple that was built in a day?" asked Barnheart

"Yes," said Petra. "The rocks told me how to do it. They were young when they were shaped. The ancients had a quarry, a sacred mountain of stone they mined and shaped to build their most holy temples."

"The rock was beautiful, full of gems and precious stones," said Yorgi.

"We found some more of the stone not far from here, but not as much as was used in the original temple. We had to make due with what we could find," said Petra. "It is still sacred stone."

"A sacred mountain, you said?" asked the Cardinal. "Near here?"

"Yes," said Petra. "The mountain knew it would one day be discovered and taken apart. It waited silently, long and still as only a mountain can. It concentrated holy energy for us to use. Can you feel it?"

"It does feel special," said Cardinal Jameson.

"And now we have this temple," said Petra. "All fresh and new."

"But for what purpose, children?" said the Cardinal. "Another tourist attraction?"

"No, for the crystal," said Petra. "We built it as a home for the crystal, just like it had been used before."

"Now they don't have to worry about activating it. The crystal will be safe inside here."

Chapter 20
A Life Rebuilt

Manny stared at the broken pieces of the airship. He had removed most of the supplies from inside the passenger cabin, spreading them out on the nearby lawn. There were tents and lanterns, tools and clothing, food and scientific instruments. He found communication equipment, several types, but none of it seemed to be working.

He wanted to explore the city. The mystery of the missing people remained, and he hadn't forgotten the goal of the mission. But there seemed to be other priorities now.

The dolphin were calm, accepting of their situation. It looked crowded for the three of them in the confined walls of the tank. He imagined they were hungry, anxious to return to the open sea. There was a canister of fresh fish in with the supplies, and he took some out and tossed them into the tank.

"I've found an aircar," he said to them. "I'm going back to the Village to get some help. With some anti-gravity devices we can lift this tank out of the wreckage and take you to the ocean. I also need to report to the Think Tank. They'll want to know what happened."

Manny went outside and prepared to get into the aircar.

"Wait," called the Cardinal, rushing towards him. "They'll be here in a minute." Before he could explain it to Manny, the children came running across the grassy plain.

"Good. You're here," said Manny. "I can take one or two of you in the aircar if you'd like to come with me."

Chapter 21
The Fate of the People

Cameron Singh felt a strange affinity with the temple. She seemed to know a lot about it, intuitive knowledge that came from somewhere deep within her soul. As she wandered the passageways she could easily read the messages on the walls. Curious about how they got there, she ran her fingers across the surface. The hieroglyphics were etched into the walls, part of the stone itself. *Of course*, she thought. *These are not painted. Petra must have asked the rocks to help reveal the sacred messages.*

She explored the outside plateau at the top of the structure. There were stone figures in four corners that served as pillars that supported the roof. The overhang created shade, and she looked out from between the pillars. She could see over the treetops and into the jungle. The surrounding city of New Maya City of Worlds was still and quiet. The only activity was around the broken airship. Cameron watched from a distance as the Gorgofsky twins worked their magic again. The crystal airship was reforming before her eyes.

"Soon we'll leave and go back to the Eighth Day Village of the Sun," she said aloud. "I don't have much time here."

"No, you don't." said a voice beside her.

Cameron turned to see a man clothed as an Aztec farmer or something similar. "I know you," she said. "We've met before."

"I am Ixpetz," he said. "I am you in another incarnation. We met searching for the Temple of the Sacred Jaguar."

"Yes," she said. "I remember now. I also met an ocelot there." The figure of the Aztec shifted, now clothed correctly as he was in life, a young Toltec warrior wearing a Cueitl skirt and a short sleeve shirt called an xicolli.

"Yes, you met my guide and mystical teacher called Oxylotl." said Ixpetz. "You learned a lot from him in that temple, but now we must go further. The people of New Maya are trapped inside the Point of Departure, and we have the knowledge needed to free them, or at least give them the choice to stay, return, or move on."

"I was trapped in there myself," said Singh. "When I returned, I looked like this." She did a little turn, making it obvious that the man she once was had been changed in more than body. "I met with our soul in a peaceful garden. It appeared as a golden being and told me that I was an instrument of my higher self, something the soul had been perfecting for thousands of incarnations to create. Being a woman now and in this time is part of my soul's plan, not mine." Singh let out a deep sigh. "I counted for nothing in this mix. Me! A reincarnated Atlantean. Why? I was perfect. I was a man, strong and confident. I faced the world with my shoulders back and my feet planted firmly on the ground. I did amazing things."

"You still have all those qualities," said Ixpetz. "Only one thing has changed. And as a woman you will find your gifts again. You need some time to settle into your new role."

"Why?" asked Singh again, looking towards Ixpetz more for sympathy than understanding.

"Please don't make this about you, Cameron Singh," said Ixpetz. "These Oversouls have their own goals and motives. Respect that, at least. Let's focus on the unfortunate souls trapped inside the Point of Departure."

"But what about me?"

"I will debate you later, but for now, concentrate on the trapped souls," said Ixpetz. His voice carried a hint of anger and impatience, so he tempered it with

130

compassion. "Believe me. If I could move the stones and reactivate the crystal, I would do it. But as a spirit I have no effect in the physical world. Please. I can't do this without you! I need you. New Maya City of Worlds needs you."

The thought of being needed snapped her out of her daydream for a moment. It is said that humans are at their best when things are at their worst. The memories of the morning, of finding out that the entire population of New Maya was missing, of her attempt to astral travel here, it all moved to the forefront of her brain. She had come here to help, and now was the time to deliver on that promise.

She remembered her own experience in the Point of Departure, a confused meeting with her soul. She wondered how many others had been transformed like her and Barclay McKenner. The only way to find out was to bring them back. Maybe, with their help, she could find a way to change back into what she once was.

Ixpetz could read her thoughts. "Why would you want to go backwards?" he asked.

"Two steps forward, one step back," said Cameron.

"The dance steps of life." Ixpetz laughed, a contagious giggle that soon infected Cameron.

"Thank you," she said, calming herself. She took a deep breath. "Okay Ixpetz, I'm listening now. Go on with what you were going to say."

Ixpetz smiled. "We don't realize it from our limited perspective, but when we improve our life in our present incarnation, it improves all of our incarnations. Your anger and frustration also affects me."

"How does that work?" asked Singh.

"Time does not exist from my perspective," said Ixpetz. "And we are all one being, whether we realize it or not. Why not think of yourself as the new, improved Cameron

Singh?"

"Okay," said Singh, not really agreeing but agreeing. "Now, what can we do for the trapped citizens of New Maya?

"My father, our father, was a priest here. He taught me everything he knew, even though it was taboo. I know, we know, how to operate this temple."

"Operate it?"

"Yes," said Ixpetz. "It is more than an observatory. It is a place that can open spiritual realms, something beyond drugs, beyond what we encountered at the Temple of the Sacred Jaguar. Using sacred drugs takes people into the higher dimensions one person at a time. After the experience, they return to the physical world, even though they are still focused on the spiritual realms. The Ascension Crystal moves the masses. Drugs are temporary. The Ascension Crystal is long lasting and can be permanent."

"And you're saying this crystal controls the doorway?"

"Like many crystals, it can be tuned to different frequencies. It happened to be tuned to the Point of Departure when it was activated."

"And that's how the entire population of New Maya City of Worlds disappeared? Except, based on what you're saying, they never really disappeared. They were just transported to a higher dimension."

"Now you get it," said Ixpetz, "The crystal was activated when the work crew dug it up and exposed it to sunlight. All that radiant energy activated its purpose. Now, you must activate it again, except this time carefully and in reverse."

"What do I have to do?" asked Cameron.

"The openings," he said. "They each have a tuning stone, a gem that channels the outdoor light into the

132

temple. When they are turned in a specific direction, they will gather the energy from the outside and channel it into the chamber that holds the Ascension Crystal."

"Ixpetz, my son," came a voice. "You cannot do this alone."

Another figure appeared beside Ixpetz. He wore the decorative garb of a Toltec holy man, a xicolli and a cueitl decorated with gemstones and gold inlays. His spirit was bright and the jewels on his cueitl glowed with their own life force.

"Father!" said Ixpetz. "Papaitl!"

"I came because I know what you both are trying to do. It will take all three of us working together to reactivate the temple."

"Who are you talking to?" asked Singh.

"My father is here," said Ixpetz. "He was a high priest at this place. He will help us activate the temple and bring the people back."

"Why can't I see him?" she asked. It was another thing that frustrated her. *I should have the power to see him*, she thought. *I'm a reincarnated Atlantean, after all.*

"It's okay," said Ixpetz. "Things work like this sometimes. Don't be concerned. I am your connection to him, and he has the knowledge we need. Let's get to work."

Together they navigated the deep passageways of the temple. Large stones with finely polished, mirrored surfaces were strategically positioned throughout. They were located near shafts that led to other mirrored stones which made a connection between the light coming through the open windows and the deep inner chambers of the temple.

"We start at these windows and direct the sunlight on a path to reach the crystal," explained the old man to his son. Ixpetz in turn told these things to Singh who, living in the three dimensional world, could manipulate the stones and make the adjustments. "Now we must go to the chamber where I will show you how to tune and direct the crystal."

At the heart of the temple they stood before the Ascension Crystal. It dominated the center of the room, it's mass pointed upright. A cloth was draped over it. "Tell the priestess to always keep it draped in the cloak of darkness when not in use," said the old man.

Singh turned to Ixpetz. " I think I hear your father," she said. "He warned us to keep the crystal covered."

"Yes," said the young warrior. "That is what he said."

The old man continued. "Unseen problems can occur if this is not done."

"I think I know the consequences," said Singh. "Now, how do we bring back the people?"

"The crystal can be turned. There are markings etched into the stone on the floor around it. Do you see them? They represent different frequencies. The crystal is balanced on a fine point deep under the foundation of the temple, so it is easy to turn. Use the handle attached to the base and rotate it until it aligns with the correct markings."

"How do I know what the correct markings are?" she asked.

"The instructions are on the walls," said the priest.

Singh noticed the glyphs explaining the temple, illustrated with pictures and writing. Again, these were etched in stone, fresh and readable, untouched by the hand of time. "The twins have done their job well," she said.

"I know," said the old man. "I watched them work. I have been here for some time, watching everything and waiting for the moment I would be needed. Now, I am going to tell you where to position the crystal."

Singh followed the instructions, rotating the massive stone with ease. By some trick of design, it was perfectly balanced and she moved it with little effort. Suddenly, there was a flicker, and like the tail of a firefly, it grew and faded until it became clear and steady. The form of Papaitl, the sacred priest and father of Ixpetz, was suddenly standing there. As he spoke, Cameron could hear him plain and distinctly.

"The crystal has helped me to tune to this dimension," he said. "And also attune you to me. Now, we must let in the light, but it too must be carefully adjusted." The high priest now explained that there were stones that needed to be moved. Along the walls there were grooved troughs, large circular stones set in them like wheels stuck in a furrow. Ixpetz pointed and stood beside his father directing Singh to move the stones by rolling them down the grooves. Behind the stones were openings. Light suddenly filled the room. The crystal began to glow. Ixpetz and his father began chanting a prayer, the sound of the words creating an atmosphere of power and austerity at the same time. Oddly, Singh seemed to know the song too, and after hearing it for half a minute, he joined in chorus with them.

It could have been the music, or maybe the Crystal itself, but something had changed. Cameron Singh was no longer angry.

"I found that even after death, I had a connection with the crystal," said Papaitl. "I have been dwelling in the heavenly fields, yet I felt something when the crystal was activated. With the help of ascended masters, I returned to this place only to find the crystal unearthed and the temple in ruins. I was not surprised to see the city empty. A similar event occurred centuries ago when we Toltecs decided to use the crystal to escape the Conquistadors and ascend. Ours was a conscious choice. For the people of New Maya City of Worlds, it was something different. Now that we have corrected things, it is time for me to leave."

"What about the temple?" asked Singh.

"Ixpetz's father reached inside his heart and pulled something out. It was a glowing miniature of the Ascension Crystal, ghostly and semi transparent. He placed it in the heart Cameron Singh, gently and with love, as if he were planting a seed. Singh glowed for a minute, then slowly returned to her physical state.

"What was that?" she asked.

"It is your responsibility now. The temple. The crystal. You are the High Priestess."

"Ridiculous," said Singh. "I am no such thing."

"You deny yourself?" said the old priest. "You look like the High Priestess of the Temple. You are wearing the vestments of the High Priestess. You have been performing the duties of the High Priestess. And you will continue to do her duties. Such is the will of your soul."

"Our soul," added Ixpetz.

The old priest shifted. His son became transparent. Smiling, he merged with his father becoming one Being. That Being glowed, turning a golden color as its skin flowed like molten metal. When it stopped, Cameron Singh was looking at his immortal soul, a golden being that had been his guide and his master throughout this whole process.

Singh stood in shock. There was no arguing with a ghost, let alone your soul. She looked down at the skirt she was wearing. It was a cueitl, similar to the one Papaitl was wearing, decorated with ornate jewels and inlaid gold, the clothing of the caste of priests.

"I don't want to be a high priestess," she said.

"Would you rather be a wife and serve one man rather than a thousand?" asked the golden soul.

"It's not that," she said. "We sacrificed humans and took out their hearts as offerings to the gods," she said. "I don't want any part of that."

The golden being shifted back into the form of the old priest. "Then don't embrace it," said Papaitl. "I didn't. Neither did Topilzin, a king who also rejected the sacrifices. He worked miracles. This temple was never used for sacrifices. It was only to house the crystal and for teaching the wisdom of the Gods. There is no sacrificial alter at the top of this temple, only an observation deck. The practice may have gone on throughout the empire but never here. Human sacrifice was used by the corrupt priests to control the people. They eliminated their enemies by sacrificing them. They made the villagers wage war on their neighbors to increase their influence and territory, feeding their spectacle of sacrifices with the hearts of the conquered tribes. They accumulated wealth in the form of gold and precious gems, things that are not meant for priests who should be attending to spiritual matters and not the things of the flesh.

"So you see?" said Papaitl. "You are not a corrupt priestess. You can make things better."

"But..."

"Listen to me, to your soul. You are now the voice of Quetzalcoatl and the bride of K'uk'ulkan," said the priest. "Ixpetz and I will be available when and if you need us. We have great faith and hope that you will bring our teachings and knowledge from the past to this world of hungry seekers. You will come to understand the crystal, my daughter. It will teach you what you need to know. You will build the City of Light and bring the people together in love."

The phantom form of Papaitl began to fade. "Wait!"

called Singh.

"We ascend," said Papaitl. "We hold the door open for those who still wish to return. The temple has served its purpose. Go. Close the Light windows and clothe the crystal once again."

With those words, he once again turned into a golden being and disappeared.

Singh felt alone. Her heart was hollow and empty. She took the dark cloth from the floor of the ascension chamber and put it over the crystal. Then she rolled the massive stones along the walls back into place, plunging the room into relative darkness. She wandered through the temple, closing windows and sealing passageways behind secret doorways and entrances, protecting the entrance to the ascension chamber. At the end of her labors, she returned to the observation deck at the top of the temple.

Papaitl was right. There was no sacrificial alter on the top of this temple, no sloped table with its carved channels to carry away the blood. No pit to cast entrails and waste into. Looking out over the lawn she could see Manny in the distance, loading the supplies back into the airship. In another direction, Barnheart was wandering through city with the children, gathering information.

"They will be leaving soon," she said aloud.

There was a gentle hum, something between the flutter of an angel's wing and the sound of a leaf vibrating in the wind. With that, people began to reappear, at first as spirits, then as solid figures, once again under the control of gravity and Mother Earth. Life came back to the city.

"They will be disoriented and will require help," she said. She could feel the maternal instincts take over, or was it the will of her soul? "Whatever," she said. "I am needed."

138

Chapter 22
Empty Houses, Empty Hearts

Barnheart was about to board the airship, but he begged for a few more minutes. Manny was glad to oblige. The dolphin were comfortable and he was again focused on their primary mission. "Might as well check the City out while we are here," he said, giving the team the okay to wander and explore.

Barnheart poked his head inside yet another house. It was the same everywhere, abandoned meals with plates of half eaten food, broken objects, work in progress. The streets were littered with quiet carts and wagons without drivers, some off the road and lying crooked against a tree or fence.

In a heartbeat it all changed. People began to reappear. At first they were disembodied spirits, phantoms that you could see right through. Gradually they became solid. Some returned to work as if nothing had ever happened. Others wandered or lay about disoriented and empty, wondering where they were. Confused family members left their houses and meals behind, joining the growing crowds milling in the streets.

You could not mistake the look of awe and respect, the subtle smiles, the quiet hearts. Each had been changed in a special matter.

"What an opportunity," said Barnheart,

"What do you mean?" asked Yorgi.

"I need your help," he said. He took off his backpack and retrieved recording equipment from it, giving it to the children and keeping one set for himself. "This is the perfect opportunity to collect data. We must conduct exit interviews, debriefings, and gather the experiences of these souls. Come, my little scientists. Time to go to work."

It was not long before they had set up a recovery center using folding chairs and camping tables. Petra took on the role of an intake coordinator, asking a few simple questions before directing them towards private areas where Yorgi and Barnheart were listening and recording their stories.

Not everyone was willing to share.

As Cameron Singh began to walk among them, she wondered how many of them had been repurposed and changed in form like herself.

It was difficult to tell. She approached an open area where people were being questioned. A few New Maya psychologists had joined Barnheart and the Gorgofsky twins creating a busy center for the population to process their experiences. The waiting area was gradually filling with lost souls.

"I was piloting an airplane that I kept trying to get back on course," she heard an old woman say. "The ground below looked like nothing I had ever seen. It was purple and yellow, not green and blue like the Earth. I knew I was somewhere else, maybe in a dream. Of course, I know nothing about piloting an aircraft."

"I saw my mother," a young man said. "She died in childbirth bringing me into the world. I met her there, wherever or whatever that place is or was. It took on the appearance of a nursery stocked with diapers and baby supplies. She told me many things that she longed to share with me. I had the feeling that her spirit had been beside me all along, following me through life ever since I was an infant."

A little girl was crying, clutching a ragged doll for comfort. Petra was consoling her. Between sobs and tears she told how she had become aware of her infinite past. For all practical purposes, she was an adult trapped in the body of a child. The tears were for her lost childhood and the passing of her innocence, torn and discarded from her life like confetti. Her inner conflict centered around gender issues and trying to reconcile her past memories in light of her current situation.

"This is my husband," Cameron heard a woman say. "I was with him in the Point of Departure. I called him a mangy dog and this is what happened." Singh could hear the fear and regret in her voice. "I didn't mean it. Is there a way to reverse this? I want him back. I want my husband." The dog beside her whined.

These and other words continued to drift up to her ears. As she mingled, Singh began to recount her own experience, rebuilding and cementing it in her mind.

Maybe what happened to me is not so bad, thought Singh. *I have my wits about me, my memories and my sanity at least.*

There was a voice in her head. "You have more than that," it said. "In time you will discover everything I have given you."

She recognized the voice immediately. It was the soothing sound of the Golden Being, a message from her soul.

A sense of contentment fell over her like a soft rain. Acceptance and trust in her higher self followed. In a moment of certainty, Cameron Singh surrendered unconditionally and accepted what had happened to her. For an evolved being, there can be only one way to live.

We all seek the guidance of our higher self. What we do when we find it is a matter of free will.

Or is it?

Thoughts continued to fill her consciousness. *The present is all we have to hold on to. The past is gone, the future uncertain and unwritten. Dwelling on the past robs the present. Ignoring the past robs the future. The only answer is to live in the present moment.*

She breathed in the scent of the air, took in the color of the trees and plant life, and felt the pain of the people as their stories continued to spew forth like so much vomit.

"They will be okay," she said. "We'll all be okay."

Living in the present moment is the only way to live.

Finding an empty table in a quiet nearby setting, she took a seat and motioned to Petra. "I'll take the next person in line," she said.

Chapter 23
Return of the Archons

Manny expertly piloted the airship. The emergency operations manual helped fill some gaps in his knowledge, but he had help. Cardinal Jameson stood beside him in the cockpit. There were only three other passengers with them, aquatic mammals resting quietly in a tank of tepid water. Barnheart and the others chose to remain behind and help with the recovery of their sister city.

From within the dolphin tank, Barclay McKenner continued to guide him as he struggled to operate the ship. His human voice was slowly fading, replaced with dolphin squeals and chirps as he occasionally struggled with the words. The growing confusion over language was slowly becoming problematic. Barclay McKenner was losing his humanity. Manny could only guess at what he might be gaining in its place. Humanity is not always cracked up to what it should be.

As he approached the Eighth Day Village of the Sun his communication equipment became active. He radioed ahead for coordination and support.

Manny's first priority was to get the dolphin back to the sea. As the crystal ship came over the mountains it was seen by all, a curiosity that caught the attention of almost every villager and tourist within sight of it. As it settled near the beach a crowd gathered. Christine was the first to greet him, wading through the shallow water overflowing with excitement.

"You're back," she said.

"It took longer than I expected," he said, reaching out with a hand to help her aboard.

A team of veterinary specialists arrived, animal health experts that were every bit the equal to their human counterparts. Barclay McKenner received proper treatment for his wounds.

Amanhatayotep and Valencia were the first to leave the ship. They did not want or wait for a check up or a visit with the vet. Instead they swam a comfortable distance offshore while their friend was attended. As people and children approached them, they moved farther away from the crowds. All attention seemed to be focused on Barclay as the specialists carefully removed him from the tank and set him down in the shallows.

Peace officers arrived, creating a barrier between the crowd and the first responders as the work continued to progress.

"We'll take it from here," said Kransky, the Village's most famous and well known peace officer.

"Okay," said Manny. "I'll get this ship back to the hanger. It's been through a lot." He pat the dashboard lovingly.

Kransky smiled.

"Can I ride along?" asked Christine. "I've always wanted to fly in one of these."

"Of course," said Manny, taking up the controls again. He looked down at Barclay and nodded. "I think I can take it from here."

Christine looked at him and smiled. "I didn't know you were an animal lover. You treat those dolphin like they were human."

"If you only knew," said Manny.

The Cardinal moved back into the passenger compartment, allowing her to stand beside Manny. "I'll strap in here for the rest of the trip," he said. He stopped beside the open door and made the sign of the cross, uttering a prayer for the soul and health of Barclay McKenner.

The crystal ship began to lift off, floating up into the sky with the ease and silence of a child's toy balloon. Manny twisted knobs and fingered the controls as the ship rose higher and higher. Christine let out a gasp as she looked down through the transparent crystal floor and at the receding landscape below them. Manny turned the ship landward again, becoming a curiosity as it flew back over the mountains and towards the storage hangers.

Soon enough, Barclay McKenner was bandaged and released. Applause rang out from the crowd, a show of hands in appreciation for what the vets had done. With a flap of his tail, McKenner turned and swam out to sea. Valencia and Amanhatayotep were waiting for him, leaping playfully around him, giving the crowd one more thing to applaud.

In the crystal ship, the Cardinal sat silently listening to the conversation from the cockpit.

"A dance as old as time," he whispered to himself. He muttered another prayer, this time for the health and well being of Manny Dubois.

"May you find what you are looking for, my friend."

Chapter 24
The Think Tank Reunited

The wall monitors in the air conditioned conference room continued to cycle through images of New Maya City of Worlds. The earlier images portrayed an eerie and empty city but these new images were full of life. Vehicles were moving and the rivers of people were once again flowing. Many of them were from the Eighth Day Village of the Sun, there to help their Sister City in this time of need.

The members of the Think Tank sat staring at them. "You can look all you want, but you won't see Cameron Singh," said Cardinal Jameson. "She moved into that pyramid the twins built. She has become a recluse, working on some kind of mysterious project."

"I still can't get over it," said Darius. "Cameron Singh is now a woman, and Barclay McKenner is a dolphin. Even after hearing about your experiences in the Point of Departure, I'm at a loss at how to explain these things."

"Nearest I can figure is: we owe our lives to Barclay and the dolphins," said Manny. "They rescued us and somehow, using their high frequency squealing and the power of their bodies, they opened a door back to this world."

"Are you sure you're in this world?" asked the Cardinal. He looked off into space. "The park where I found Cameron Singh was as real and as solid as any place I'd ever been to. It was a perfect replica, just like my office, even the building I was in. Exactly the same." He turned to Randall. "I touched the furniture, I felt the heat from the fire in the fireplace."

"Yes," said Manny. "Even though my reality kept changing, it felt and looked as real as anything." He looked off into blank space for a moment. "If only I could remember it all."

"I've seen Barnheart's preliminary reports," said Randall. "He, as well as many others, agree with you about the reality of the Point of Departure. As far as your memory goes, most of the people have regained that knowledge. I expect your memory to return soon."

"Yes," said the Cardinal. "I remember everything. You will too."

Manny went back to staring at the wall monitors. Every now and then he would catch an image of people doing nothing, just sitting outdoors, vegetables ripening in the sunlight. He couldn't read their minds but he imagined they were contemplating and processing their experiences. It reminded him of afternoon visits to the nursing home to see his aunt when he was a kid. Inside his own mind, he could identify with them. It seemed that, like the people on the monitors or like his senile old aunt, a piece of him was still missing too, lost and left behind somewhere. If he went back, could he find it again in the Point of Departure?

Is it important to find these things again? If only he could remember what he had lost, then maybe he would know what to look for. Until then, he would have to live with this feeling of being incomplete.

"Well," said Randall. "I must say, it is good to see you all here. We are what remains of the Think Tank. We are down quite a few members."

"Yes," said Darius. "Juliana is content to stay with her husband in Washington DC. And Nan Chi Han remains in Africa with the warlord Kenji Alamoto."

"She and Alamoto may be destined for marriage as well," said Stine.

"She is doing wonders for agriculture, affecting not just Kenji's empire but the entire continent," said Randall. "Our efforts to build sustainable gardens and feed the world continue to grow as fast as the food crops they plant."

"Yes, also thanks to Mel Ewing, another missing member of the Think Tank," said Manny. "Isn't he there in Africa as well, overseeing the construction of these gardens?"

"Yes," said Darius. "Lately he has been teaching others how to build them. His mission should be complete soon. He'll be back after that."

"That still leaves us with these vacancies," said Randall.

"Why not keep Barclay as a member?" asked Manny.

"Meetings may be difficult," said Stine.

Cardinal Jameson spoke up with an idea. "Why not use modern communication software to network all these..." He struggled for a word. "Beings together for your meetings?"

"We tried that," said Stine. "We found it best to meet in person. Members who are absent are usually focused on other activities. It's best to let them stay focused. Besides, it is our combined energy that makes these meetings productive."

"Not to mention the problem of time zones," said Manny. "Can you imagine waking up in Africa in the middle of the night just to attend a meeting?"

"Which is why we have that rule," said Stine.

"You know," said Manny, an afterthought erupting in his mind. "His forte was human dolphin communication. Why don't we facilitate that?"

"What are you saying?" asked the Cardinal.

Manny piped up. "Should we build a water tank in here, like the one in the crystal ship?"

"Great idea," said Darius. "Why don't you look into

that?"

"I second that," said Stine,"

"So moved," said Ravi.

"Next order of business," said Randall. "I see no other option but to fill some of these these open vacancies in the Think Tank, even if it is with temporary members." He looked toward Manny.

"Agreed," said Darius. "Do you have anyone in mind, Baba?"

"I do," he said. "I'd like to nominate Cardinal Jameson as our new spiritual advisor."

"Me?" said the Cardinal.

"Why not," said Manny. "You were invaluable during this last incident. I was glad you were along with us."

"I second the motion," said Stine.

"I must agree," said Darius. "Despite my earlier reservations, you have proven yourself an asset to this group, Your Eminence."

"Thank you, Darius," said the Cardinal. "I must accept the job then."

"Good," said Randall. "What about you, Manny? You've been a temporary member for a while. Have you decided yet to make it permanent?"

Manny blew an empty breath of air. He looked off into the distance.

"We need you," said Stine. "This is twice that you have risen to the occasion and managed to pull success from the jaws of disaster,"

"Come on, now," said Manny. "I had help on both occasions. Particle physics alone did not stop the hurricane. And without the team that volunteered for this mission, well, I don't know how things would have turned out."

"You could still teach at the research center," said Stine. "And there's always the bistro when you get bored."

Manny laughed. Through the fog of memories, he felt himself back inside the Point of Departure.

He heard the voice of a woman, laughing along with him as she said, "Keep looking for me. One day, when you give up your search, you will find me."

The voice came from deep inside himself, echoing from the end of a dark tunnel.

"So, you'll make the leap?" asked Randall, bringing him back to reality. "Come up here full time?"

"Or are you still interested in finding the next Mrs. Manny Dubois?" added Darius.

Manny remained silent before saying, "That doesn't seem so important anymore."

"Good," said Randall. "Then it's official."

"Don't be so hasty," said Manny. "Let me think about it some more."

"Fair enough," said Randall.

"What about Singh?" asked the Cardinal.

"I'll contact him." Darius quickly corrected himself. "Her." He shook his head. "Sorry." He took a deep breath. "I'll see what Singh wants to do."

"Yes," said Randall. " Based on initial research, things changed dramatically for everyone involved in this incident."

"Amen to that," said Cardinal Jameson.

"Well, that said, before we adjourn, are there any more questions?" asked Randall.

"Yes," said Manny. He cleared his throat. "Actually this is more of a question of etiquette and protocol than something to do with the Think Tank. It's been bugging me."

"Okay," said Randall. "Ask away. We're the Think Tank and we will share our opinions."

There were nods of agreement as all eyes focused on Manny.

"My question is: Do you think it's okay if I continue to hit astral Singh now that she's a woman? I kinda still need my solid proof."

Chapter 25
I Shall Singh No More

"Thank you for coming to see me, Cameron," said Randall. "I know you have your work in New Maya, but as a member of the Think Tank, I need your personal debriefing. I'm trying to comprehend everything that happened. Please take a seat."

The exotic woman sat with such grace, it was as if every motion was practiced. It was not just the movement of her body, it was the added smile, the swirl of fabric, and the simple toss of her hair as she settled into the chair.

"You seem to be adjusting well to being a woman," said Randall.

"I have no choice," said Singh. "And I would be a fool to be untrue to myself."

"Yet, inside, are you not still Cameron Singh, reincarnated Atlantean?"

"Cameron Singh is still here," she said. "I have his direct memory and experience. He is me and I am he. And I am still a reincarnated Atlantean, nothing has changed there. I can still access all my past lives, astral travel, and do everything I used to do, maybe even more."

"Then explain it to me," said Randall. "What happened in the Point of Departure? Why are you a woman now?"

"I told you, I had no choice." She looked off to the side, staring out the window and at the sky. She saw clouds in the distance, seeing past and through the air that surrounds everything. Yet, it is there. You can feel it, sense it, breathe it. Unseen forces of temperature and pressure are only the beginning. There are also the winds of change. If our invisible atmosphere can do all that, what about the psychic and the higher dimensional worlds that also surround us?

She looked back at Randall. "Let me start at the beginning and go back to the time before New Maya disappeared, before I reported in to the Think Tank that day. I was late because I was meditating. In my recent meditations, I had been meeting my soul in a peaceful garden."

"Interesting," said Randall. "What did your soul look like?"

"It appeared as a golden being, Buddha like, wise and peaceful. We met and spoke often, sitting on comfortable benches next to a trickling lotus pond. That was also where we met in the Point of Departure." The memory came easy to her. She closed her eyes, seeing it vividly in her imagination. "Yes, there were birds, chirping melodies like nothing heard here, even in the jungle treetops. And the scents! Floral fragrances like no other. Talk about aroma therapy."

She opened her eyes. "It was just like my meditation, only real. The bench, the pond, the flowers. Everything."

"Yes," said Randall. "Real. Just as the others reported."

Singh continued. "I was disoriented that morning when I arrived here. My soul had been criticizing me in my meditation, telling me things, deep and personal. Things that disturbed me. The peaceful garden did nothing to comfort me. Eventually, my meditation was interrupted and the visit with my soul ended abruptly. That's when I saw the message from the Think Tank on my communicator and reported in."

"You came in person," said Randall.

"Yes, still feeling a bit off. I was having trouble getting back into the meditative state that I needed to astral project, otherwise I would have done that to report in. But after walking the short distance to the conference room, I became focused again. When I arrived you asked me to astral travel to New Maya City of Worlds and I agreed. I seemed to slip easily into a deep state. I went over the mountains and above the jungle, heading towards the city. Then it happened. I was glad that the Cardinal was watching me. I understand my body disappeared completely."

"Yes, it did," said Randall. "That's when we sent an expedition after you."

"That must have been the moment I crossed the threshold," she said.

"Threshold?" asked Randall.

"Yes. The doorway to the Point of Departure," said Singh. "As I was flying towards New Maya, I thought of my friend Anton as a point of reference to be drawn to. It helps to have a focal point when astral traveling. A destination is a destination, be it a person or a place." Singh smiled, enlightenment glowing on her face as she realized something.

Randall saw it too. "What is it?" he asked.

"And then we met again, in the Point of Departure," she said.

"Yes," said Randall. "The mysterious realm created by the Ascension Crystal."

"Anton was already inside the Point of Departure," she said. "Naturally, when I focused on him, I was drawn there too. That's why my body disappeared. That's how I got there. It wasn't so much the crystal. It was me."

"Yes. More about this crystal," said Randall. "Is it safe? What's to keep this all from happening again?"

"The crystal is fine. It's been surrounded by the temple and placed in alignment with the energy fields around it. The dimension opened when the archaeologists at New

Maya unearthed the crystal and exposed it to direct sunlight. The solar energy activated it, and without the temple to contain it or the priests to control it, the crystal did one of the things it was designed to do. It opened up the door to the Point of Departure."

"I understand the temple is being rebuilt," said Randall.

"It is built already," she said. "The Gorgofsky Twins did in a day what it would have taken months, maybe years to accomplish with our present technology. The temple has been restored and rededicated, like new again, complete with materials found in the jungle. There is a certain stone they used, laden with gems, and it sparkles when the sunlight hits it right. At night even, I can look into these stones and see the stars reflected back at me. It's as if each gem embedded the stone contained a miniature universe."

"I must come for a visit and see these things," said Randall.

"Yes. Yes," she said. "Please come. The city is empty. Nearly two thirds of the population of New Maya decided not to return."

"You mean, they are gone?"

"Not gone. They just departed for a different destination than their lives here on Earth."

"So. They had a choice," said Randall.

"Exactly," said Singh.

"And you say you didn't," said Randall.

"That is correct," she said.

"Explain it to me again," said Randall. "I might have missed it the first time."

"As I was saying, I met my soul in the Point of Departure, in an environment that mirrored the meeting place in my meditations."

155

"Cardinal Jameson said this garden where he found you, it was the same as a garden where he used to meditate. It was next to his office in Vatican City."

"That may be so," said Singh. "Or maybe not. It is hard to say what really happened in the Point of Departure, except that by our own perceptions, we each had a unique experience."

"Such is the nature of perception," said Randall. "Go on, please. What did your soul have to say after you met in the Point of Departure?"

"We had a discussion, and my soul thought I was too ego based."

Randall sighed.

"What?" said Singh

"I would agree," he said.

"Then why didn't you ever say anything about it?"

"I thought you said it all with your 'I'm a reincarnated Atlantean' speech every time you opened your mouth," said Randall.

"I was stating a fact, not stroking my ego," said Singh.

"It didn't come off like that," said Randall. "It sounded more like a statement of superiority. Words acquire intent by the inflection of one's voice. In that way they can inadvertently transmit emotions with them."

Singh huffed. "I am aware of that."

"Even now, it bleeds through," said Randall.

"What bleeds?" said Singh.

"Listen to the way you said 'I was aware of that'. Did you not detect the hint of superiority in your voice?"

"I am proud to be a reincarnated Atlantean," said Singh.

"Perhaps too proud," suggested Randall.

Silence filled the space between them, as invisible as the air. "It seems my soul agrees with you, Randall." Another moment of reflection followed before she added. "This change is supposed to help me with that."

Randall put things back on track. "The Cardinal said he found you in this meditation garden, that the dolphin rescued you."

"They did," said Singh. "I wouldn't have thought it, but they were essential to the mission."

"Do you think Barclay McKenner becoming a dolphin had something to do with the rescue?"

"Barclay certainly knew the way out of the Point of Departure. It was he who led the dolphin team."

"Yes," said Randall. "What did you do after leaving the Point of Departure?"

"I was drawn to the temple at first," said Singh. "There, I was contacted by one of my past incarnations who showed me how to operate the temple and use the ascension crystal."

"How fortunate," said Randall. "Without their guidance, the doorway to the Point of Departure would have remained open. Any idea what the affect of that would have been?"

"Yes," said Singh. "I believe that the citizens of New Maya would have remained trapped. Another day and we would have lost more. It would have been quite easy to move on to another destination. All you have to do is think about it, maybe find the exit point that would take you there."

"Fascinating."

"We were in a dimension where we had complete control over matter, able to manifest it physically in any form we needed or desired. I daresay there are still some souls there playing with this concept, with this self created reality. It didn't matter if you were conscious of the world you created or not, your mind was making it happen."

"Yes," said Randall. "I'm eager to hear people's stories. The exit interviews conducted by you, Barnheart and the others should prove interesting."

"Yes, they should," said Singh. "Well, that's it. That's my story. Any more questions?

"Not really, except maybe, what do you intend to do?" he asked. "You are still a member of the Think Tank."

"I'll have to resign. My work is in New Maya," she said. "The Crystal calls me, even now. The City, like its residents, is being reborn. We are trying to create a spiritual haven on earth, a physical manifestation of the sacred city of Shamballa. Do you know how Las Vegas is known as the city of sin? People go there for liquor, gambling, and pornography. We want the opposite, a City of Light where people come for life help, healing, and spiritual practice."

"Then I wish you luck, Cameron."

"Thank you, Randall," she said. "You are still our sister city." She stood up to leave. Her jeweled cueitl skirt was eye catching, as was everything she was wearing. "One more thing. Cameron Singh is in the past. I must embrace my future. I will no longer go by that name. I am now Kamala Singh."

"Kamala?" asked Randall. "Isn't that another name of the Hindu Goddess Lakshmi?"

"I see you get the reference," said Singh. "I didn't want to be overt and name myself directly after the goddess, but it more closely aligns with who and what I am now."

"Yes," said Randall. "Lakshmi is she who leads to one's goal. She is a mother goddess."

"A Supreme Goddess!" said Singh. She shifted her weight from foot to foot. "Like me, she has beauty, wealth, fortune, and purpose."

"She is also associated with Maya, who represents illusion," said Randall. "I daresay you are setting yourself up for another bout with ego."

"What makes you say that?"

"The way you said *Supreme Goddess* with such emphasis," said Randall. "It seems the same way Cameron Singh used to say *Reincarnated Atlantean*."

She looked down at Baba Randall. *Righteous holy man*, she thought. *What do you know of being a goddess?* She smiled, but Randall could see beyond it. One cannot question the motives of the soul, but in this case, it does open up the subject for lively discussion.

Randall heard the same words in his own mind, whether received by psychic impression or not. *What do you know of being a goddess?* It was a silent question he had for Kamala Singh.

Singh pulled her priestess cloak around her with a feminine twirl that was not lost on Randall. Cameron Singh was larger than life, and Kamala is no less his equal.

And with that, the astral form of Kamala Singh disappeared, leaving Randall alone.

"Well," he said. "This has certainly given me a lot to think about."

159

Chapter 26
Goodbyes

Franklin Van Dorn paddled in the water beside the boat. The three dolphin circled around him, chirping happily. Van Dorn tried to smile, an outward happiness that masked his sadness.

The dolphin sensed it. They offered a distraction by playing with him, but knew it would not sustain him. He was suffering with grief, the loss of his friend, Barclay McKenner. Like all grief, he would have to work through it and get to the other side by himself.

He climbed back aboard the boat, empty and forlorn. McKenner had been the first friend he made in the Eighth Day Village of the Sun.

The dolphin continued to gleefully circle the boat.

"This is going to advance dolphin human communication light years," said Van Dorn.

McKenner poked his head out of the surface of the water and nodded.

"I know," said Van Dorn. "I can almost hear what you're saying. *Existing in any state, any form of consciousness, results in learning.*"

The dolphin nodded again.

"How could you do this? Who am I going to talk to now?"

There were chirps and stutters.

"Oh, right. I don't know about him. Darius is a bit of a... I don't know. I can't find the word I'm looking for."

McKenner let out a long squawk.

"Well I wouldn't exactly use that word," said Van Dorn.

He snorted. "I heard you still had a human voice."

Barclay nodded.

"Then why don't you use it?"

The dolphin shook his head.

"Yes, yes," said Van Dorn. "As long as I can keep guessing what you are saying and pretending we are having a conversation, you don't have to say anything."

McKenner nodded.

"Okay, then. If that's the way you want it."

Another nod.

"All right, my friend. The afternoon breeze is coming up and the sea is getting choppy. I have to head home." He looked down at the dolphin. "Unlike me, you are already home."

McKenner laid on his side, splashing water at the boat.

Van Dorn started to laugh. "Is this crazy or what?" he said.

Valencia and Amanhatayotep leaped into the air, landing on their backs and sending water into the boat.

"Hey!"

The three of them stood up, their tails shaking as they broke through the surface and rode backwards across the water.

Van Dorn laughed again. "Okay," he said. "All tricks aside, I'll see you tomorrow."

There were nods of approval from the wet set.

Van Dorn grabbed the wheel and started the engine as the dolphin swam off. In his imagination he wondered what it would be like to live in the sea and explore it.

The mountains towered in the distance, visible far offshore where he met his friends. Eighth Day Village of the Sun grew larger on the horizon as the boat drew closer to home port. Despite the beautiful day, he remained solemn and quiet, thinking about everything that happened. He wondered what his life would be like as a dolphin. He thought about it a while, then dismissed it as crazy and absurd.

"It might work for Barclay but it's certainly not for me," he said.

He docked and began tidying up the boat, storing gear and coiling line. He took a cloth and wiped down the rub rails and the console. He was about to leave when he heard someone call his name.

"Franklin?" said a woman's voice. "Franklin Van Dorn?"

He turned to stare at a beautiful woman, close to his age, dressed casually for an afternoon at the beach. She held a gear bag containing a mask and flippers.

"I'm Van Dorn," he said. "What can I do for you?"

"I understand you do dolphin research," she said. "More than a few people in the Village told me about you. I'm interested in what you're doing." She snickered. "Your research, that is."

"Oh," said Van Dorn. "I see." He had trouble finding words. "What exactly were you interested in?"

She held up the gear bag. "I'd like to join you for one of your day trips if I may," she said.

"I'm done for today," he said. He thought about inviting her tomorrow, but he couldn't find the words. What would she think about him? Talking to dolphin, claiming one was his transformed friend. He'd have her running for the hills or calling the men in the white coats. He turned away from her, trying to look busy as he fiddled around with some loose rope as he tightened the dock lines.

"I won't be any trouble," she said.

He stopped fiddling and turned to look at her. "What

are you trying to accomplish?" he asked.

"I used to work at the Seaside Aquarium in Florida," she said. "I was a dolphin trainer. I quit to go to college and get my doctorate degree."

"In what?" asked Van Dorn.

"Marine Biology, of course," she said.

He went back to fiddling. "A useless degree," he muttered.

"What about you?" she asked, trying to make a connection. "What's your degree in?"

"I'm an MBA," he said.

She laughed.

"What's so funny?" he asked.

"I don't know," she said. "I'm just trying to figure out what that has to do with dolphin. Do you handle their business affairs?"

He laughed with her now. She was utterly charming the way she asked that question.

"I'm their banker," he said. "I once worked for T. Harmon Rothschild, richest man in the world. Now I work with dolphin."

"Then their finances must be in good hands," she said.

There was a pause before he asked. "Have you eaten yet?"

"I'm hungry, if that's what you mean," she said. "This was more important than food."

"What? Meeting me?"

"Yes," she said. "What about it? Will you take me with you tomorrow?"

He reached into the boat and grabbed his gear bag. In a brief moment, she had made him forget all about his grief and his missing friend. Normally, he and McKenner

163

would go somewhere, eat and talk about their day at sea.

"Why don't we discuss it over dinner," he said.

She smiled. "I'd like that," she said.

They began to walk down the dock towards the Reiki Spa and Resort. "They have a good restaurant here," he said.

"I know," she said. "I live here too."

"Oh," he said. "How is it I've never seen you about?"

"I haven't been here that long," she said. "Maybe you could show me about?"

He nodded, a smile replacing his mask of gloom.

"That would be great," he said. "I could use a new friend."

"So could I."

Chapter 27
Manny Happy Returns

The sun fell below the horizon and as the night canopy appeared, a dense fog covered the Eighth Day Village of the Sun in a cool, moist blanket. Manny followed a familiar path from his apartment to the beach. Bright lights did nothing to reveal the path ahead except, like stars overhead, they helped him navigate and find his way.

He wasn't doing anything in particular, just wandering around trying to clear his mind of so much detritus.

He found himself at the entrance to Manny's Beachside Bistro. Inside, a woman sat at a stool leaning against the bar sipping a drink. She was the only person there. "About time you got here," she said. "I'm tired of self service. I need some personal service."

"Christine?" he said. "What are you doing here?"

"I don't know. The weather is foggy and nobody is around. I came here hoping to find some action, but this place is dead."

Manny instinctively went to the bar, standing opposite her on the other side of the counter. "What can I do for you?"

Without a word, she leaned forward. Before he could react, her lips met his, wetting them with a warm, deep kiss.

There was no resistance. He returned the kiss, as passionately as he could.

"Now that's what I call service," she said, her hand pressed to the back of his head, refusing to let him stop for long.

She finally released him. "That was nice," he said. A

slight sense of *deja vu* overcame him. He pulled back and looked at her, his mind groping for answers.

"Thank you for the ride in the crystal ship," she said, filling the void with conversation.

"Sorry I had to leave so abruptly yesterday morning," he said. "Can I make it up to you?"

She smiled. "Of course you can." She slid off the stool and walked over to the entertainment center. He followed her every move, watching as she turned it on and selected something to play. Music began to fill the bistro, a soft, romantic bossa nova. "How about a dance?"

She held out her hands, inviting him closer. He came out from behind the bar. Manny met her touch, electric current flowing through his body like lightning through a ground rod. Her touch held the promise of passion. It wasn't long before she was in his arms and they were spinning and dancing like they had been partners their whole lives.

The music played on. He held her hand, expertly letting her twirl wildly about him. She was no amateur, and her movements were as fluid as anyone who studied and worked hard. Manny was not without his moves either. He found it remarkable that he could read her next move and act in such close harmony with her.

"Where did you learn to dance like this?" he asked.

"I could ask you the same question," she said. "But does it really matter? We are dancing, after all."

"Yes," he said. "You're quite good, you know."

She smiled, spinning into a pirouette. "Thank you."

"Trained in ballet I see."

She did another spin, as graceful as anything he'd ever seen.

"Are you a professional dancer?" he asked.

166

"Oh," she said, her words exaggerated. "Are you asking me a question? Something personal you want to know about me?"

"Yes," he said. There was that sense of *deja vu* again. "I do," he said hesitantly. "I want to know more about you."

"Since when?" she asked. "I've been here all week and you haven't asked me a single thing about myself. You know nothing about me Manny Dubois, and yet I know a great deal about you."

"Really?" he said. "And what do you know about me?"

"I know I'm the perfect partner for you." The music stopped and she drew closer. "Do you believe in love at first sight?" she asked.

"I believe in a lot of things," he said nervously. "Yes. That happens to be one of them. And what makes you so certain that you're the perfect partner for me?"

"Because I'm the one you've been searching for."

"Who says I'm searching?"

"Don't be coy," she said. "Stop with the bartender act. I know you like me. Get rid of that little bit of doubt you harbor about sleeping with a woman. You tell yourself everyone wants to sleep with the bartender, but nobody wants to marry him."

"Caroline was not like that," he said.

"Face it, Manny, Caroline's not coming back," she said. "You're stuck with me." She continued to look at him, a gaze that held him captive for the moment. Her movements became slow and seductive.

"I'm demi-sexual," he said, trying to slow her down. "I need a strong feeling before I jump into bed with someone."

"Then feel this," she said.

She kissed him again. Her felt a connection,

something stirring deep inside of him. *Is she the one?*

He heard a woman laughing in his head.

He looked up at Christine. "Actually, there are a lot of things I'd like to know about you. The real you, not the person I imagine you are."

"Ask me any question and I'll answer truthfully," she said.

"Is that so?" he said. His voice held an element of whimsy. "Any question?"

She laughed. "Okay," she said. "I set myself up for this."

Manny cleared his throat. "Would you like to take a walk on the beach in the moonlight and talk some more?"

THE END

We hope you have enjoyed reading this novel. For other fine books, visit our website at halfabook.com

Nick Delmedico is an award winning new age writer. His work includes *Tales of the Lightworkers*, *The Seven Day Marriage*, *Aliens vs Dinosaurs at the Beginning of Time*, and the Eighth Day Village of the Sun series about a futuristic intentional community (*Free the Giraffes*). You can reach him on LinkedIn and at halfabook@dplus2.com

Also by Nick Delmedico:

The first book in the Eighth Day Village of the Sun saga. In the future we will have intentional communities, villages and cities based on humanistic ideals. They exist today, places where people choose different values to live by. Eighth Day Village of the Sun is one such community projected into the future. Set beside the sea, the village has embraced spiritual and humanistic values. They are led by Baba Randall, a holy man who hears of the collapse of nations beyond the walls. Civilization is breaking down. Riots, shortages, war, and coups abound. A contingent of leaders is headed his way asking for help. Not all want help, some are ready to steal technology to maintain their control over the world's population. Will spirituality win out over the banal?

The first novel in the Aliens vs. Dinosaurs series. Sixty five million years ago giant beasts fought each other for dominance of the herd. One monarch has a vision of a better world in which dinosaurs cooperate and live in peace. But that peace is shattered when hostile aliens from another planet challenge the dinosaurs for dominion of the Earth. They collect the small ones, the children, taking them away to a distant laboratory where they can experiment on them and find new ways to destroy the dinosaurs once and for all.

King Rex finds his daughter is among the missing. As his world crumbles around him, as his enemies circle around him looking for weakness, he struggles to find a way to harness the power of flying without wings. His goal: to send an envoy of peace to the aliens and negotiate the release of the children. Failing that, to take the children back using an army of dinosaurs that have united behind him with one thought in mind: Rescue the children.

This book was a 2017 Human Relations Indie Book Award Gold Winner. In 2014 Nick's wife was diagnosed with end stage esophageal cancer. He saw her through chemotherapy and radiation treatments, but it was not enough. Three years later when the cancer returned, metastasized in her lower gut, she refused treatment. He and his son left their jobs to take her on a final bucket tour. This is their story, a family driving towards an inevitable destination that cannot be avoided. But if you live bravely, there can be many pleasant stops along the way.

A little angel in heaven asks her father: "Do angels die?" He knows the truth, having survived the great war that separated Heaven from Hell. His brother Lucifer expected him to take sides against their Father, putting him in a moral dilemma. He instead joined the neutral angels, undertaking a mission to carry the Holy Grail out of heaven to a place of sanctuary in a sacred mountain. Thus begins a momentous quest through heaven and hell and all that lies between. He will cross-rugged terrain unknown to man; pits of fire, caves of darkness, and fallen angels out to destroy him and his band at every turn. Throughout this ordeal, one question keeps surfacing, a terrifying thought that he fears to face. "Do angels die?"

www.ingramcontent.com/pod-product-compliance
Lightning Source LLC
Chambersburg PA
CBHW051519170626
46811CB00002B/903